# To Give and Receive with Grace

K.G. WATSON

ISBN: 978-1-989506-34-9
www.pandamoniumpublishing.com
pandapublishing8@gmail.com

Dedicated to Lacey Bakker


Whose encouragement and skill made this and
other books happen for the enjoyment of so many.

# BOOKS BY K.G. WATSON

Duty's Dad
Duty's Son
Duty's Daughter
Life Supports
From One Christmas to the Next

Available at www.pandamoniumpublishing.com/shop

1

It was just too damned cold to be out these days. Instead of sharing coffee at the entrance to the riverside walk, the guys decided to meet at the warehouse in the New Year. The one where Winston had been hiding when the women's trafficking mob moved in next door.

Tatters of crime scene tape fluttered from the door-frames at that end of the building; large padlocks secured the doors. Winston directed the guys to an entrance into the other half of the building. The metal sheeting behind a pile of pallets would swing sideways and let you in. Because the trailers that were evidence had to be kept as they were, the heat was turned on at minimum levels - enough to keep them from freezing. When that system went into operation, it also warmed the separated section where the Company of Homeless Men now gathered.

As they straggled in, Jacob and Winston greeted them and pointed to the coffee and day-old donuts. The scuttlebutt of where each person was staying and how they were getting on was shared. Had anyone found a job? "Who was missing and why?" got passed around. Winston got many laughs when he described how Jacob had asked what kind of living space Winston would design for himself if he could.

"Well, just like this," Jacob had said, waving to his three-bedroom bungalow. "He didn't offer to give it to me, but he didn't kick me out for being a smart-a… smart aleck," he corrected himself. Everyone laughed before Winston went on. "He gave me a place to stay when nobody else would. But he's got an idea he wants to share with you guys. His head's in the clouds most of the time, but his heart is in the right place. Give him a listen. He's serious."

Jacob was glad to see Winston had saved out a large box of donut holes and one of the carafes of coffee for the latecomers. Jacob served it out in half cups to make it spread.

Winston caught Jacob's eye and nodded. Jacob raised his voice.

"Thanks to you all for coming! We've gone to great expense to hire this hall, and we have to be out before the police find we're here."

There were chuckles all around.

"I'm here to update the project you heard about at the party back at Christmas time and maybe since then. The idea is that it would provide housing, training, and safety for men - any of you who might like to join it. As we've talked lately, you've made very clear what you'd like to change about the places in which you now live. I've taken those ideas to the people who will finance the project, and they're on our side. The head honcho built the place for battered women. You know the big tower?" Everybody nodded. "They've already started turning official wheels to make a place for homeless men a reality. They tell me that once the plans are approved, it could take two years to complete. So that's why I'm here. I'm the messenger for that organization. They have an offer." People waited silently but attentively.

"We're talking about two years from now; they want you to be living in your own apartment in a high-rise beside the other one." There was muttering about what they would do in the meantime.

"I already told them that we needed a more immediate response, and the following is what has been worked out. It's a good news-bad news story; here it is.

"Each apartment unit will be built on the ground by the man who will occupy it. That construction can start before this Easter - a couple of weeks from now. With that effort on your part, the plan is that the project could be completed faster.

"So here is the offer, and in two weeks, it will be commitment time. If you want in, that will be the time to step up." Some men looked over their cups at him with narrowed eyes; others stared at the floor. They'd been tricked many times. Was this another sham?

"Each of you will work with the skilled trades to create your own place - so you don't injure yourself - and to be sure the place meets code and the building plans to work through the system. Some of you already have those skills but might have dropped out before you got your ticket. Here's the chance to pick up that process. And we'll need you to help those who need to learn how to do everything." Silent shuffling filled the space.

"Your apartment will be three hundred and twenty square feet. It will be cozy and will be built from shipping containers." The crowd burst out laughing.

When they settled a bit, he shouted over them. "Well, that's where some of you are living now, isn't it?" There were some knowing nods, and some looked away. "But these are going to look like luxury trailers by comparison. These will be heated, air-conditioned, and you will have the key to the lock on the door. Here are some pictures." He passed around some photocopied sheets. "You must share the photos," Jacob insisted.

The echoes in the warehouse sounded happy. "Sure, sign me up." "Who wouldn't want something like that?" Others shook their heads. "What's the catch?" Eventually, someone called out over the crowd and everyone waited to hear the answer. "What do these things cost?"

Jacob waited until silence had settled. "These things will cost your soul." The statement brought complete silence. Jacob was shocked by his own blasphemy, but it was too late to recall it. He dashed on before anyone laughed.

"The easy part of the cost is the labour. Under skilled helpers, you're each going to build your future house - or a start on it. You won't start to earn a wage from the project until you've 6 finished your own apartment. After that, you can earn apprentice wages or wages appropriate to your training if you've got the skills already. That is the easy part."

"But you must agree that the needs of the many overrule the needs of any single person. If you're going to be part of this community, you can't start a grow op or do drugs. You've got thieving in mind? Leave now. This needs to become the safe place you all seek, and it needs to be a model of cooperative social behaviour. We need to create, together, those rules that will govern all, and you will need to follow them if you want to remain in the group." There was nervous muttering.

"We're at the end of the time we booked," Jacob continued. "Think about what I said. I think we can build a community that could be a model for a lot of other places. If you don't want to join, there is no problem. We still want to meet with you. But we're not going to talk about the bedbugs at your place, how you haven't eaten for a while, or what job you got kicked out of because you weren't qualified. Solutions to all that is what you can have in the company of your friends if you decide to join the team. Talk to me about any questions you have."

The group broke up into pairs and bunches. Jacob headed for the singles. Pete, the beer can collector, was one. "I don't know how to build things," he said quietly. "And where would I keep my buggy and cans?"

"There will be a special lock-up for your cans and buggy. Only you will have the key, but it will be for one shopping cart only - not in your apartment. And if you have trouble building what has to be made, you will have all the help you need to make it. In fact, you might get someone else to do work for you while you do another job that is important on the worksite. Maybe you could be the tool dispenser and collector of cut-offs. Believe me; you will save us so much in material. They'll make you a foreman."

Pete rocked back and forth a bit. "OK," he said. "Can I go now?"

"Where did you leave your cart?" Jacob asked.

"Outside, behind the barrels."

"You're in? I can count on you?" Jacob pushed.

"OK."

"Be careful. Snow coming tonight," Jacob warned.

"Yeah."

Jacob expected him to shuffle off as he usually did, but he stood for a moment, rocking his head as though he was waiting for the conversation to continue. Jacob was about to ask what he wanted to talk about when Pete looked up at him and smiled. It was the first time Jacob had seen him smile.

"Thanks," Pete said and headed for the door.

The reaction caught Jacob completely off-guard. For all Pete's fixation on beer cans and bottles, Jacob thought he'd had the first peek behind that veneer. It was as though Pete had a side he'd never seen. "Wow," he thought.

Winston, meanwhile, was in deep discussion with a cluster of men who obviously had misgivings about the project. It was clear; he was playing the listener. He'd wait till they vented their frustration about the communal demands of joining. In fact, he was urging them on with a comment that floated out. "So, you like where you're living, eh? Fixed the leak in the ceiling, have they? Is the shared toilet down the hall working now?" To another, he asked if elevator 8 was working yet. "Still have to walk up? That's a long trip, eh?" Jacob knew the man lived on the eighth floor.

One man standing apart seemed to be waiting for the industrial overhead heater to come on. The circle he walked was in the downdraught. Jacob had noticed him on the street and at their meetings only in the last couple of weeks. He approached the man and put out a hand. "Jacob Eiger."

"Dan," replied the heavyset man with his hands thrust deeply into his parka pockets... he did not extend his hand. The heater blew into action far above, and Dan held his face to it.

"I haven't had the chance to talk to you before," Jacob opened.

"I arrived in town after Christmas. Everyone is talking about the dinner you hosted. I just came for the coffee and company this morning. What's this about the housing plan?" Jacob outlined the opportunity to build a small personal apartment in their project.

"I'd have trouble with some of the handiwork." He held

up the piece of a hand that came out of his pocket. "Got it caught in a press on my last job. Safeguard didn't work. Didn't take off enough for me to get a prosthesis. He held up his thumb and baby finger that gave him a pinching action. Hurts like hell in this weather." He stuffed it back into his pocket.

Jacob wasn't going to dwell on the injury. "You have much experience on a shop floor?"

"Well, I can read drawings and follow directions. It's just really hard to get a job with what they call a 'pre-existing condition.' Lots of others who are able-bodied are in the same lineup."

"Sounds like you might be looking at retraining in something else."

"Jeez, that is a hard prospect. Been a long time since I was in school."

"And the alternative is ….? I can tell you there are many like you here. I think you can help each other and build something others will be lining up to hear about. Maybe we could put you on the lecture circuit. You can probably get a feel for something that might make you financially independent if you chose to. That is for another day. Today, all you need to decide is if you want to put your hand on that door and open it." He tried to save what he thought might have been a social gaffe by asking, "Does your injured hand open doors?"

The heat roared out of the unit overhead.

"Well, as I said, it has only closed doors for me lately."

"Maybe time to use it the other way. Come for coffee next week," Jacob invited. "Got a place to stay in the meantime?"

"Yeah, I got a room at the Y. It's close to the employment office. I go there every day."

"See you next week?" Dan nodded.

"Good luck," Jacob said and waved. Dan waved with his good hand.

2

"The construction plans are working their way through official channels," Maggie declared when she met Jacob in the elevator. "Someone has to be sure that a water pipe drawn entering one side of a wall comes out on the other. I'm sure there are historical precedents at the root of the practice, but it sure sounds like a power trip on their part."

"Maybe it's like doing the instrument count before you close up the incision," Jacob suggested. That harkened back to Maggie's status as head nurse in the surgical ward before she inherited the fortune and became the heiress who had created the sanctuary for abused women.

"Probably correct," she sighed, "but it seems to take an extraordinary length of time. How many men are signed up?"

"We're stopping at forty-five for now. That is all the space we have on the site to build apartments and still leave space for the construction. I'd forgotten that the dwellings needed to be connected to bathroom facilities and dining spaces. Glad to have the engineers looking after those things."

"Surely each apartment has its own bathroom?" Maggie

said.

"Of course, but on the ground, it is easier to connect to the municipal system if we back ten apartments around a single unit that provides shower and toilet facilities for all ten residents. From that, there is a single connection to the mains. When each apartment is hoisted into place, it will connect to its own pipes up there, and the private facilities can go active. This communal thing is only needed as an interim measure on the ground. Maggie had her hand in the elevator door to stop it from closing.

"Keep me posted, nice to see you again. Keep up the good work in the classroom." She was gone, and the door was closing before Jacob could reply.

Since he had been defrocked as a minister for advancing liberal theology in the conservative community that had hired him, Jacob's job was to teach critical thinking and philosophy to the children who came with the abused women into Maggie's shelter. The rule was 'no religion.' Maggie had explained how the religious communities from which the women needing her help had escaped, usually subjugated women, so they all got banned. 'Give and accept help with grace' was the summary for the way things went. And they celebrated the solstices and equinoxes instead of all the religious festivals. It seemed ironic to him, but it was her house, so her rules.

So Jacob fell back on the Greek philosophers to illustrate the critical thinking skills that were his mandate. It had been a challenge to adjust the content to the age range, but the teenagers helped the younger students as part of their training in the social expectations of the community. It had worked out well for his first year; now, he was expanding the curriculum.

When a parent had accumulated the job skills and the nest-egg needed, they were expected to graduate from the community to leave space for the newly needy. So children graduated to public schools when their moms moved out or headed to college and university if their moms were still in residence and they had outgrown the school. Other students kept arriving from traumatic backgrounds with histories of abuse and evasive practices learned under them. It was a chaotic mix, but Jacob had floated along in it successfully for one year with his program. He seemed to be making good headway with the encore performance.

As he walked down the hallway to his classroom, he had to confess that last year's lessons on Socrates and Diogenes might have been too successful. It was the reason he'd decided to take a mathematical bend this term. Pythagoras was on his mind, and the recent cease and desist order issued to the children about their digging in the snow piles along the parking lot had settled the idea in his head - three parts. First it started with the snowdrifts.

The BIG snowfall a couple of weeks back had led to the piles along the parking lot - some over fifteen feet high. They became instant slides and subsequent tunneling exercises that stopped only a day ago when parents began to worry about the catastrophic risk of collapse. But for Jacob, it was a made-to-order lesson plan. His shoulder bag held the starting parts - a box of stuff: six cubic blocks about six inches on a side and six small drills. He'd tried to get more but had to settle for the three small battery-powered ones and three of the old manual kind. Each drill had a quarter-inch twist bit, four inches long.

When everyone settled, he announced the challenge. He held up coloured lengths of cord. "When a team gets their cord through the block, they get to go for ice cream at the mall on Saturday afternoon." Since he started the reward plan, it had been a favourite. "Each team gets a drill, a drill bit and a piece of wood. Please work on the planks that are on the tables in the middle of the room. We must not damage the furniture. As soon as you have your hole, come and get a cord to prove the hole goes in one side and out the other. To qualify for the reward, all members of the team have to have helped do something. He ticked off the points on the green board as he said them.

It took a while to figure out how to load the bit into the drill, but as soon as that was mastered, the expectations leapt. Punch the drill through the block. Easy. Then the drills bound in the hole and stalled. After the first group figured out how to drill a short distance and back the bit out to clear the shavings, the rest caught on. Not long after, and with the drill chuck pressed against the wood, it was found that the drill bit had not come out the other side. It was too short.

He called the end of the exercise before frustration at drilling from the opposite side got out of control. Soon he was calling the time and directing the return of the equipment. "Keep your blocks and get these skewers when you return the drills and bits. And pick up Smarties from the bowl for your group."

One group sent their smallest member to claim a cord. When they brought back their tools, their block had a string through the hole on one side and out through the adjacent side. It was strung along that side and into a second hole that also cut across the corner of the block and out the side opposite.

"I want you to put the skewers into the holes you drilled from opposite sides, then look from the side and top to see how well they line up." The groups quickly saw how misaligned their holes were, and that's when they saw how the successful group had managed to accomplish their task.

"But that's cheating," some complained.

"We just thought of a better idea," the successful students bragged. They knew they had aced it. "We did what was asked, so we should get ice cream on Saturday."

"Well, they did accomplish the task," Jacob observed, "just in an unconventional, even unexpected way. Look at the board. Did they do what was required?"

There was gradual agreement if grudgingly given.

"See you on Saturday then. We'll gather in the dining room at 2 PM," Jacob announced. "But let's get to the point of the lesson. First, it was hard once you had to come from opposite sides. Right?" Mutter assented. "And second, it was solved by something unique."

"So here are the notes to put in your notebooks, and one of the points makes the focus of our studies important.

The focus is a man named Pyth…ag…o…ras, and he lived in a town that did just what you tried to do to bring water to their town from the other side of the mountain; only they were successful. They actually dug a hole just over a kilometer long," he paused "that's the distance to form here to the Mall, through the mountain BUT," he waved his hands theatrically, "they dug from opposite ends of the tunnel at the same time. See the problem?" He drew a picture on the board.

Everyone saw that the tunnels would likely miss each other. "How the two tunnels managed to meet so water got to the village was one of the ancient wonders. They managed it because they used something pretty unique." He looked at the successful group. "They used mathematics."

"They might have used the trick our friends here used, but they didn't. They punched in from both sides, through limestone, hacking away with picks and hammers, and the tunnels met. Can you imagine how happy they were on that day when one broke into the next? And they didn't even get ice cream." Everybody laughed.

"It is even more remarkable. Not only did the tunnels have to meet, but one had to slope down, the other upwards slightly over their distance so that the water would flow by gravity through the hole. It couldn't just run in and not out. So there was a right-left perfection and an up-down perfection that had to be met."

"Oh, and one more thing," He waited dramatically; scanning to be sure he had every eye. "It had to be done in the dark! Tunnels are very dark. Torches might help, but no flashlights."

He returned to the ban on mining of the snow piles outside. "The people in our story hacked their way through solid stone. You were digging in snow out there." He waved to the window. "There is a serious risk of it collapsing. That is why you can't do that anymore. You could die, and it would happen in a blink. Nobody could get you out fast enough. So stay safe and admire what those ancient people did. They used their heads, and because they did, they had water for their town."

"These people had a fascination with numbers and what they could mean. Numbers even worked in the underworld, which made them even more magical. Pythagoras grew up in that environment, so that is another part of our lesson. Your environment matters." He wrote that on the board. "He also became a super teacher - so super in fact, that we remember his name thousands of years later."

"Let me put him on our timeline." The line still carrying the children's names, his, Diogenes and Socrates from a year ago, was still drawn down the wall from the front to the back of the room. Jacob added a bend that let it continue across the back wall of the room. "On the line here, is about where Pythagoras was born - in 570 BCE." He made a mark and added the name and date. "So Diogenes and Socrates knew all about him when they were in school."

He had to review the concept of getting older and the years getting smaller in number. He used the student suggestion from last year. "It's like a count-down clock."

Again it seemed to work as long as you didn't leave too long for them to think about it.

"As I said, Pythagoras was a super teacher - so good that the school he founded went on for centuries. Many children, even adults, came to learn and went on to be famous on their own, so it became a problem in present day to decide who really did all the things that Pythagoras was given credit for. Was it really Pythagoras or one of the graduates of Pythagoras University who did them? Lots of confusion there, but Pythagoras' name sticks on a mathematical relation that fascinated everyone back then and still does today. Maybe Pythagoras discovered it, maybe not, but his name is on it. It is called the Pythagorean theorem, and it evolved into a way for builders to be able to get perfect verticals or perfectly square corners. While I write it down, you put the other notes in your notebook."

When they had finished, so had he, and he read his statement from the board. It was in coloured chalk. "The square on the hypotenuse equals the sum of the squares on the other two sides." Complete silence met the pronouncement. "You all need to memorize this. Say it together." And they did, raggedly and slowly, with him.

They repeated it more times, each time picking up the pace just a little and saying it a little louder - rote learning at its best. Finally, Jacob held up a hand for silence. "And that statement means …?" Blank stares.

"It was a secret password. That's why you must not forget it, but it comes with a memory aid, and that is THREE, FOUR, FIVE." He wrote then numerals again in coloured chalk. "Watch this."

He drew a long horizontal line on the board a bit above the chalk trough and put a big dot near the beginning. "I'm measuring three lengths of my index finger." They watched him. "Now I need someone to measure four and then five lengths of my finger lengths on this string." He set it on the desk and asked two children to hold it tight while a third marked off each space with a marker. Kids at the back had gotten up from their seats to watch what was going on.

Holding the end of the string at the start of the one on the board, he scribed an arc of four fingers radius. He drew a second arc of five fingers radius to intersect the first arc from the other end. He made sure everyone agreed that each point along each arc was the same distance from the centre and went over it with the string lengths. Everybody got it.

"Now, here," he pointed to where the arcs intersected, "is the point that is four fingers distance from that end and five finger lengths from the other end. Right?" He got guarded agreement.

With his meter stick, he drew straight lines from both ends of the chalk line to the intersection and stepped back to admire the formed right-angled triangle. He went over the construction to be sure each person accepted that the sides were the actual number of units, writing them as he did.

"Here is the magic," Jacob whispered. "This thing measures angles. He held up his large protractor for use on the blackboard and slid it along the horizontal line till it was over the vertical arm of the triangle. "A perfect ninety degrees," he announced, pointing to the number. "A ninety-degree angle means that if the bottom one is perfectly horizontal, then the upright one will be perfectly straight up." Builders needed to know how to get perfect verticals if their buildings were not to fall." Scrunched faces were wrestling with the concept of crooked buildings.

"Similarly, if you had a perfect vertical, this three, four, five rule let you find a perfectly horizontal, and you needed to know that if water was to flow down through the tunnel. The tunnel had to tilt a bit below the horizontal at one end and be dug upwards, heading across the horizontal by the same amount at the other in order to meet. So let's go over that again." And he did.

"Homework is to draw at least five new 'three, four, five' triangles using different units. I used my finger. You can use your fingers, your shoe, or the desk size; any unit you want. Here is some string, markers and an angle measuring thing called a protractor. Come and get them after you have finished making your notes."

3

Jacob and TD were in the parking lot after school ended for the day, and the engines on the fans were roaring. Slowly the enclosure was inflating. It would cover a soccer field when the season began. They had rented it to temporarily enclose the work area where the men would be insulating and applying exterior cladding to their homes-to-be. Once that was done, the shipping containers, which is what each home had initially been, could be moved to the habitation area and hooked up to the city services when the tower was built to receive them. As long as the containers were secure against the weather, the men could work inside without a problem. It was now getting to that state which required enclosed, dry space.

Getting the men to buy into a community was another matter. But if that didn't happen, all the rest would fall apart. Even though TD, who had taken over the logistics of outfitting the shipping containers as homes, wanted to talk of nothing else, Jacob had to keep returning to what the men thought about the rules to live by. TD had been in the military at one time; it was why he was living on the street now. Couldn't deal with ordering men into harm's way and getting them killed. But he had organizing skills up the wazoo.

"What do the guys think of the photograph idea as part of the site security?"

"No big deal really when you realize how many cameras we pass on a day. And they all dressed up for their photo at Christmas. That's not nearly the issue that adult female companionship is. If you think this is going to be a monastery, think again."

"Have you any idea what went on in monasteries?"

"Don't care, but the idea of forbidden cohabitation with girlfriends, even getting married, is a show stopper."

"But won't the apartments be too small for a couple, let alone children?"

"I'm glad you brought that up because I was thinking on how two adjacent apartments could be linked with a ceiling unit over the wedge that would separate them as single habitations. By the time you add another hundred plus square feet, you've got a seven-sixty in the combined place, but that opens the door to permanent residence in the tower. Is that what you want? If they move out, you have to train replacements into the way of living there".

"That was one of the purposes in the first place - to prove that a community focused on common consent and purpose could actually happen in this world that only seems to know selfishness."

"Maybe part of the plan should include permanent residents that hold the values and make the community attractive so that outsiders will give up being self-focused and will realize that it's what they really have been looking for."

"Another day's discussion, I think."

\*

The buzz went round the streets that the next coffee meeting would be at the worksite and that their pictures would be taken as they entered in order to make up their security tags. Nobody complained about standing in front of the line of shipping containers in the cavernous space under the inflated barrel overhead with a warm coffee in one hand and a donut in the other. A cold rain was pouring down outside.

"Christ, look at them all," one commented around a mouthful. "How many of the God damned things are there?" The row in front of them was only the first of many that stretched back into the dimness.

Winston was behind the loud-mouth with a box of new donuts. As the man reached for one, Winston caught his hand. "Jake and the others would appreciate it if you left the profanity outside." The man's eyebrows shot up. The steel grip around his wrist loosened immediately. "Reward for right behaviour, eh?" and the box came closer.

"Shit, if it's a God damned Sunday school class," The box that had been at his fingertips was suddenly out of reach, and Winston arched his eyebrows in a silent question.

"Oops, sorry," he replied with a short laugh. The box was now back in reach.

Jacob called them for attention. He felt like he should be starting with a prayer. The habit of his earlier life died hard. He replaced it with a heartfelt welcome to see so many had committed to the project. "So here's what's next," he continued.

"You each need a security card to get back in here. They're colour-coded, so you know who you'll be working with. We've tried to put friends we know of together. We're all doing basic work to start with, finding out how to do what's needed to get the containers ready before each of you gets your own. And there is no timeline to meet. We want this to be safe and friendly. We want everyone to give and receive help with grace."

"Who's Grace?" the loud-mouth blurted.

Nobody laughed. A couple turned to give him a questioning look; others just said what was on their mind. "Shut up, eh?"

Jacob went right on without seeming to hear at all. "I can't overstate the need for safety here. We want no accidents. Here's our on-site medical guy. Bruce, will you step out?" The man who was at the back of the group took half a step forward and raised his hand. As he looked around the group, his half-smile softened the sharp features; the overalls hardly hid the muscular frame. "Bruce was most recently a medic with the army and joined us to make sure we're all healthy every time we step through the gate." He didn't say that Bruce was also undergoing PTSD rehabilitation.

"Maybe you've heard about the hassles we've had with some local groups who don't want you here. Any excuse will do to get them roused against us again. They want you somewhere out of sight. Congregating in the business district is not what they had in mind. Everyone is under scrutiny by a host who wants to give us all grief, so watch yourselves."

"Everyone on site must be wearing appropriate safety equipment, so before you leave, you'll each get the safety boots and socks, overalls, safety goggles, ear protection, and hard hat that is required on-site. Get work gloves as you need them. If you're worried about wearing your stuff on the street, you can change here, but you have to be in it to step through that door." Jacob nodded to the doorway.

"You'll have qualified tradesmen working with you to direct your work. The tools you'll need will be passed out to your team by Pete." Everyone knew the guy who collected beer cans and bottles. "Please do not try to put one past Pete. He knows numbers better than anyone here, and his word is law. He'll give what you need at the start of the day, and you'll hand it back, all back, before we go home. He'll also collect off-cuts and pieces surplus to your team's needs. If you need small pieces, ask him. Any questions, come and see me or TD or Winston. Line up to get your stuff. Coffee cups are in the barrel by the lineup."

"Good to see you, Pete," the first man said to the worker behind the table of overalls, stacked in piles by size. "I think I need an XL," Pete asked his name and put the scope into the box beside the man's name on his list.

Beside Pete stood Bruce handing out correct boots and other gear. The dispensing went smoothly. Nobody noticed Bruce ask one man to come around the end of the table to check the size setting on his safety helmet and the tube of special shampoo he was given only after a few words. Bruce set his pile aside and pointed the guy to the showers at the end of the change facility.

"I'm on disability for my back, man. Have you got something I can do that isn't going to screw up my workman's comp cheques?"

"Sure can," Bruce said. "You'll get these." He handed over noise-cancelling ear protection. "You'll start inside the containers, and it will be noisy. Try these." He showed him how to turn them on. "You'll hear shouts but not the other stuff. Get batteries from me daily. What's your name?" Bruce noted it on the name sheet. "Now give me the details about your claim so I can make sure you don't get blowback on your payout."

\*

It was Pete's duty to pass out the tools to each team as they entered the work area. Pete knew where any tool was at any moment, even the model and serial number of the specialty tools. One of the professional tradesmen had tried to short circuit the process to get a tool he needed. He didn't want to Pete to take it back from where it was, record it and then let the new man have it.

"That'll take forever, you God damned idiot," the tradesman had shouted, "And what difference will it make anyway. You're just a stupid retard. Get out of my way." He slammed Pete back over the worktable. The second push knocked the table into the tool shelving, which then collapsed like an explosion. It was Pete's wailing scream that brought TD on the run.

TD's ears had pricked up at the raised voices, the scrape of a table and the crash of falling stuff. It was the scream that had him reaching for the Army folding knife in his pocket as he ran, and its murderous blade was out when he came around the corner to see the bully reaching across Pete for the big grinder. Pete was cowering on the floor, knees to his chest, hands over his ears.

One of the guys had snapped up a cut-off scrap and brought it down hard on TD's arm. The knife slammed to the dirt and stuck. TD's momentum carried him forward. A left to the gut and a roundhouse right with his empty fist lifted the bully right off his feet. By then, the rest of the guys had poured onto the fighters like blankets, smothering them. Someone threw a coat on the knife and picked it up in the folds when he retrieved his garment.

Bruce the medic had been in the midst of the mix. But he was cradling Pete, whispering in his ear as though the scuffling and shouting were in another building. When Pete's wails faded, Bruce had scooped him up, took him to the first aid corner of the change room, and closed the door quietly behind them.

4

The triangle homework results, at first glance, met expectations. Jacob was looking at them as the children gathered. Variations from right angles came back to careless measuring and were another point to put in their notebooks; poor measuring produces, poor results. But he knew he could still draw the amazement of millennia past from the students in the room. There was something mystical about how it worked. He was about to start the lesson when his phone buzzed in his pocket; Jacob had forgotten to turn it off. His finger was about to shut it down when he glanced at the number on the call display. "I think I should know that number," he thought.

"Hello?" It was one of the homeless men in the work gang out in the parking lot.

"Need you immediately," said the caller. Jacob knew the voice and the tone. A riot was going on in the background. Piercing through it was a scream like he'd never heard. He could only think of it coming from one person.

He strode to the child's desk nearest the front classroom door and bent over to whisper in his ear. "David, go to the office and bring back the Principal as fast as you can. Tell her it's an emergency. Shout and scream if you have to, but do it fast." The kid was out of his seat before Jacob turned. It would be a short trip, but if everyone was busy...

"Alisha," he'd said tightly.

Her eyes snapped up at the tone of his summons.

"I need you to organize the homework. Get everyone to put it on the board - organize something helpful. Children, Alisha is in charge." He shouted to all.

The door burst open, and the School Secretary, being dragged by David, stood there wide-eyed. "Look after them," Jacob directed. "Alisha is leading the lesson." He pulled the startled woman into the room and sidestepped past into the hallway at a run. He took the fire escape, three steps at a time.

The thump, thump, thump of his steps down flight after flight, made him think of what TD had shared with him over recent weeks. Pete was TD's cross, and he could not lay him down. Pete had emptied every clip he had, keeping enemy heads down so the team under Daren's command could escape the ambush. From the relative safety of their new position, he had told Pete to retreat while they all covered him. He'd made it halfway across the road to the safety of the ditch where they all were when the explosion lifted the man and threw him right over Daren's head. Pete hit the wall spread-eagle, weapon flying, helmet spinning away and then the kid fell right behind Daren, the side of his unprotected head hitting the rock with a crack he could not forget. Darren shoulder-carried the kid all the way to the 'copter while the rest of the team poured fire on the enemy. He escaped with Pete, who was near death; the rest did not. The gunship demolished the enemy but not before the enemy took every man he had led that day into the trap he failed to see.

Pete somehow recovered, but he was never right thereafter. He'd lost the bright, happy person he'd been, the guy who was a technical whiz. It was tough to be in groups anymore - a loner who collected beer cans and bottles and knew at any moment how many were in the shopping cart that he pushed. He rarely said three words in a row, not a dozen a day when Jacob first met him.

Daren Thomas became 'Daring Thomas' after that mess, and the implication was not flattering. He was the guy who risked everything but his own skin. His moniker became DT when his alcoholic habits overwhelmed him, and he was hospitalized. He was pensioned off, managed to turn his life around and changed his initials to remind himself every day of the new man he had to continue to be. The old one was, well... he just dared not think of that anymore. He'd found Pete on the street after a long search and became his protector. It was the least he could do.

Jacob slammed open the fire escape door and sprinted across the parking lot toward the work area as fast as old legs could carry him. The white safety helmet of the on-site supervisor was visible in the middle of the group between a small shouting line of red-faced tradesmen on one side and an enraged mob of vagrants in new coveralls opposite when Jacob ran in. Jacob caught Bruce's back, heading towards the locker room. It had to be Pete in his arms. He recognized the long fingers with which the victim was covering his ears.

Jacob pushed and pulled his way to the middle, shouting as though he was calling down a deity on an apocalypse. "STOP. STOP. BACK UP. OUT OF MY WAY." The fist swinging had devolved into a shouting match that had already been losing steam when Jacob had burst in. His hysterics seemed to suck the air out of the argument further as he pushed his way to the supervisor. When he saw TD across the circle, being held hard by the others, he was sure the victim had to be Pete. The man being pulled to his feet across the area had to be on the other side of the fight.

"STOP. BACK UP. MOVE," he ordered to the white hat, who was just the engineer who happened to be on-site. "Take those men over there and see if you can get what happened from them. I'll take these guys."

Voices settled. Jacob's directions rang through the huffing and puffing like judgment through a cathedral. Already, the homeless were backing up and heading where Jacob pointed, muttering amongst themselves. He spotted Winston and stepped quickly toward him. With a hand on his shoulder, he spoke into Winston's ear. "What the H-- What happened?"

"I got here just before you."

"Can you get a story from those who saw it? I'll take this bunch over here. Write it down. Get names." He turned back to the overturned table and collapsed shelving. Pete's clipboard stuck out of the mess. Jacob snatched it up and handed half the wad of blank forms under the top sheet to Winston. Got a pen?

"Nope."

"Take this." He yanked off the one tied to the clipboard by a string. "Write on the backs." As he handed it to Winston, Jacob patted his own pocket. Pencil and pen still in his pocket protector.

He joined the bunch left after Winston drew a crowd away. The air he stepped into was filthy with profanities.

"OK, what happened?" Jacob began, and everyone spoke at once. Hands came up in supplication. "I can only listen to one at a time. Did anyone see what happened?"

Tom flicked his hand up. "Pete had just given us our fucking tools, and we were headed to our container, he pointed down the floor. I heard a God damned shouting, like screaming …"

"Guys, I'm going to have trouble if you keep swearing. I don't know if it is me or the situation or someone else being cursed. It would be a big help if I could just get the story in undecorated English." He looked back up at Tom. "Maybe take a breath. I'm not going away."

"OK," Tom continued, "There was some shouting and scuffling behind me, and I turned to see that electrical trade guy screaming in Pete's face. Pete had his hands up over his head," Tom showed everyone, "and Pete's earmuffs had fallen off. Then the guy pushed him once and again harder, so Pete fell into the table, and that pushed it into the tool rack, and that's when it collapsed. Pete was on the floor screaming like-- And the other guy had picked up the big grinder we use to smooth off the edges of where the torch cuts or to cut hatch openings."

"Yeah, that's what I saw too," Gary added. Tom waved for Gary to continue. "And then the other guy was looking down at Pete screaming bloody murder on the ground when TD came round the corner," He pointed to where the event had happened, and the others nodded.

"I never saw TD so angry. God, he was almost black in the face. I thought he had his knife in his hand; you know that war one from way back. Christ, if he had, that guy would have been dead meat."

"Can we skip the epithets?" Jacob asked, head in his hands.

"No," Hat continued, known as such because he always wore a battered top hat. He completely ignored Jacob, "TD has his fist all bunched up. He knocked the board right out of my hand. God, when he hit that guy in the gut, did you hear that? F'n whoosh. And then the right to the jaw. Couldn't happen to a nicer guy."

Jacob managed to get things calmed down a bit before he asked. "Did anyone else see anything?" Nobody admitted. "Can I get you guys to write down what you told me?" He held out the paper to the men.

"You write it down," Tom said to Gary, "I forgot my

glasses." They both laughed.

"OK. I got it, but I forgot my fountain pen," Gary chuckled. "I suppose this will do." Jacob held up the sharp pencil.

As Jacob gave the paper and pen to Hat, the man pulled him a little closer and slid something heavy into his pocket. "TD would have killed that bugger if I hadn't taken that off him," he muttered. He took the paper and pen and backed away to start writing.

5

Jacob had to report the results of the meeting to Maggie. Last thing to do before going home for a late dinner.

"I gave the document copies to legal," he began. "The executive summary is that Austin Zid, a tradesman working for the contractor, did verbally abuse and push, aka assault, Pete Mulholland, our stores master, in an altercation about the speed of service at the checkout bench. Zid, in turn, was assaulted by Darren Thomas, one of our foremen, in retribution for the aggressive action directed towards Pete."

"Both have agreed not to file suit against the other. Zid's contract has been cancelled, and he has been banned from the site. Most of the other tradesmen have quit in sympathy. I was told by one that they have to work on other projects and can't be seen supporting a project that fired one of their own, even if the guy thoroughly deserved it. We've replaced the expertise with retired journeymen and Shop teachers, but the project will slow down because of that. The residences will still be ready well before the tower will be in place."

"Don't bet on that," Maggie replied. "We've been given a big grant to build the solar collector, like the one we have here, but the strings attached say that it has to be completed by year's end. So we've been pressing the city planning department to issue permits within the month. The contractor has committed to round-the-clock shifts to meet the deadline. It means that you have two months before the bubble comes down, and the shipping containers have to be moved out of the way."

"So the men could be living in their homes by summer?"

"Well, if they get moving, they could."

"Those places will need air conditioning. That was going to be supplied centrally in the tower, but we'll need 50 separate units on the ground. They'll have to see if he can find right-sized ones to fit the hatch holes cut for the central A/C and heating or makeup templates to bridge the gaps."

"I'll pass that along to the project manager."

*

Alisha's chart of the student's work was still on the board when they met the next day.

"Did someone get killed?" the first child, with his hand up, asked.

"Where?" asked Jacob.

"On the workplace. Isn't that why you rushed out? To

administer last rites?"

"Where did you hear that?" Jacob asked.

"Around."

"Well, nobody died. Two grown-ups got into a fight when one mistreated the other. Both were friends of mine. The person who called said it was an emergency. It might have looked like someone had died, but everyone is fine now." He pushed on before the cross-examination could continue.

"Let me admire your work and Alisha's organization." He applauded alone. "I could not have done better myself. Let's all give a round of applause to Alisha."

Again he led the clapping. The teens all stood, turned toward her and gave a single loud coordinated clap and sat down. It took Jacob a moment to catch on, but he hurried on.

"Can you all see the point that this chart makes? Every triangle you made up using the rule comes out as what we call a right-angled triangle. This ninety-degree angle here is called a right angle. Please don't ask me why." Two hands fell back into laps.

Most of the kids remembered the theorem. He beat it to death again and this time added what the square of a number was and a hypotenuse and did the arithmetic to prove the point. He put the seniors together to find other similar triangle sizes, but in the end, they agreed the one he had given was easiest to recall.

"New topic - but don't forget the last one. Here's the one for tonight. It is about Circles. Using your string once more, measure the distance around a circle - called the circumference, and the distance across that circle from one side through the centre to the other - that's the diameter. Pick any circle you want but come back with five each." He had a can on hand to demonstrate how to do the task. There were no questions.

*

The circle homework results exceeded expectations in one case. Alisha returned with the diameter measurements of the cylindrical columns in the cafeteria on the top floor. She also seemed to have been the driver behind the group, which solved getting the cord through the block. The ratio's she derived from her measurements proved she had made the diameter determinations accurately. He asked if she would tell the class how she did it. They had to adjourn to the cafeteria for the demonstration.

In the lounge area adjacent to the cafeteria were long, rectangular tables that served as coffee or end tables in the conversation clusters of chairs. It took no time to push the chairs away and set the middle of one table tightly against a column. Other tables were moved to the column, so they made three sides of a box. The new tables also pressed tightly against the edge of the first that extended beyond the column.

"I measured these tables by the three-four-five triangle and found they had square corners," Alisha began. "When I pushed the tables against the side of the column and also against the first one, I thought they should measure a straight line across the middle of the post. Did I do it right?"

"What do you think, class. Is Alisha right? Is the distance between the side tables the diameter of the column?" Most of the younger students didn't understand. Some of the older ones said she might be right. Two checked that the side tables were tight against the one that made the baseline and pointed out that they would angle and make the distance between them incorrect if they weren't.

Rather than return to the classroom, Jacob said the lesson would end there. Homework was to divide the diameter into the circumference measurements of their circles to one decimal place. He would talk about the number they would all have the next day. He watched Alisha, and a couple of the older ones show the younger students how to use their calculators to do the division. Jacob made a note in his daytimer to talk to Alisha's other teachers and maybe the school medical officer about a test of her intelligence.

The next day Jacob had two photographs to start his lesson.

"Is that you?" asked one of the young students.

"I'm flattered, but no. This one is a sculpture of what the

artist thought Pythagoras looked like. The other is our man of the circle, Archimedes."

He gave birth and death dates for Archimedes and asked a tall student who could reach the timeline to put them in place. It took a moment to get the proper placement of 287 and 212 correctly on the BCE line.

"How does anyone know what they looked like?" asked one of the older students.

"Someone took his picture," another joked. He got Sebastian to repeat his answer from a year ago when the same question came up about Socrates.

"The sculptor made him up to please the guy who paid for the bust," and then went on to explain why he thought that. After the diversion, Jacob had to use his voice of authority to get things back on track.

"Here were men who, because of these constants, were convinced there were number relations hidden in everything." He got the students to repeat the Pythagorean theorem and then asked what Archimedes' value was called. No reply. The way Alisha looked at him told him she knew. "I guess I forgot to tell you. In Greek, the number is written like this '$\pi$'. It is even given a place on the computer keyboard; it is called Pi."

Of course, the children said pee when he wrote the English letters, had to be corrected, and couldn't stop their jokes for the rest of the lesson, well, until he brought out the pie and offered a piece to anyone who could state the meaning of Pi and say it correctly. Just to see if the ratio held, he asked them to measure the circumference and the diameter of the pie plate and do the arithmetic again. After food, he took them to the outside window on the other side of the hall from his classroom. There they observed what had been laid out in the parking lot below. "That is Archimedes in action," he said, then went on to explain how engineers had to compute the volume in order to order the right fan to inflate it. And they couldn't do that without knowing about Pi.

6

Just when the tradesmen left after the fight and the guys all thought they'd be spending their days waiting for direction, Jacob arrived with the bad news. The timeline had been sliced into pieces, and the order of projects had to be revised entirely.

"We have to get these things weather-tight in eight weeks. That's fifty-six days. We have to complete about one a day, and if we don't complete one on a day, we have to finish two the next. No weekends off. How can we make that happen?"

Most dithered to each other. It was Dan who put up his good hand. "If each team works the way we've been doing, it still can't happen. It just takes too long for each group to learn each new task. On a shop floor, that idea would be a non-starter." Everybody was nodding.

"If we had a list of all the jobs, maybe we could make teams of one to three that do each job on all the units. Like cutting the access hatches and service ports. If we had specialists who could handle the torches and cutters, they'd just move down the line cutting the holes. Grinders come next to clean up the edges, then the framers. If one job was taking too long, we make another team work on that so that that task stays ahead of the next." Nodding had moved to talk between pairs.

"I think that sounds like it could work."

"But it can't…"

"So you could…"

In no time, a list of the tasks was scribbled on paper, and the men had bunched themselves into teams.

"We won't have to keep checking out tools every day. We'll be responsible for our own. That will make Pete feel better. He can handle the small pieces and bring things we need. He can also look after repairs and replacement, and bring us new grinding wheels or fresh heads for the impact drivers."

"Can he check them out to our new teams, so he keeps control? I think that's important. What do you say, Bruce?"

By lunch, everyone had a new assignment. The team who measured where each cutout had to be, had already mapped out the first four containers. The waxed white lines were clear on the metal and labeled. Water, sewage, and a lightning bolt on the back wall for electrical cable, H/ AC access on the roof.

Dan climbed a ladder to see the work on the one and came back a moment later with some plans from the engineer. "Hey guys, this is a problem. His baby finger pointed to numbers on the blueprint. "This hatch for the heating and air conditioning has to be three feet from that wall and six from the back. The others looked at their work and space.

"Shit. We got it backwards. Did we do the same on all of them? Lemme see." He made to jump across the six-foot space to the previous container.

The plans fell in a mess as Dan's good hand shot out and grabbed the sleeve of the adventurer. "Please don't do that," he said more urgently than he intended. "Look." He thrust his mutilated remnant of a hand up in front of the man's face. "I look at that a million times a day, and it reminds me of the safety stop that wasn't working because the last guy was in too much of a hurry. He jammed it but forgot to unjam it when his shift ended. Yes, you've jumped puddles that size your whole adult life, but it takes only once to miss and… man, you live a long time with those regrets. And if we had a workplace accident to deal with well, it might kill this project. Take the ladder. Just come back to get us down." The tension oozed away in the face of Dan's urgent and personal plea.

The markers got busy locating the cut lines correctly and were ready to climb down when the ladder was back. "All the others are OK. The cutters are already working on the first one."

They moved on, repeating the adage about measuring twice and cutting once.

The first of the replacement tradesmen from the local community college arrived in mid-afternoon expecting to find a workforce drinking coffee and telling jokes. Pete stopped them at the door. Bruce was right beside him. "Who are you?" Bruce asked. Pete checked their names off.

The place was buzzing with activity but no running around, just purposeful movement. "We seem to have the skills mastered. Could you go around and see what you think?"

Bruce was walking around with Pete as he picked up pieces. "Look, tighten up that flame like this," said the welding instructor to one of the guys. "You don't need to heat all that space. It'll give you a smoother cut, less grinding needed, uses less gas. Yeah, that's it. Beautiful."

When they were bringing more marking sticks to the measuring team, Bruce heard the Machine shop teacher telling the guy with the grinder. He held out a hand to stop Pete so he could listen in.

"OK, stop for a moment. Look. Brace yourself like this. Jam that elbow right into your hip and tuck the other one in here. It takes the weight off your arms and gives you more control. It can kick back when it goes through the metal, and it will take off your leg faster than I can say it. Get that stance solid. Yeah, like that. OK, now hold this. Get tucked in. See? If it kicks back, it will go that way away from your body. There, OK, make it go."

On the way back, Bruce told Pete they should check with TD. He was at the radial saw notching two-by-fours for interior studs. "How're things going?" asked Bruce.

Pete was scanning for cutoff pieces. He was about to start picking up the three-quarter-inch scraps when TD looked up. "Glad to see you, man." He patted Pete on the shoulder. How you doin'?"

"OK."

"Use the broom to sweep this stuff up. I'll hold the dustpan."

Pete reached for the broom while TD talked with Bruce.

"He's doin' well," Bruce nodded. They watched Pete carefully collecting the dust and chips. "Have you noticed anything about the way this place feels this afternoon?"

"Well, busy, but now you mention it…" he cocked his head, "it feels smooth. I heard a couple of the guys laugh like at a nice joke. Not loud, but… Sort of like between pals."

Bruce related what he'd overheard on the way. "It's like the temp came down to shirtsleeves from torrid. TD shook away the thought of the last time he'd been in really hot conditions.

Hat came by to collect up what TD had cut. He'd jammed his top hat down over his safety helmet. He counted the stack. "That'll finish the inside of that box. Hey Pete, good to see you."

"Hi Hat," he replied and was about to return to his sweeping but stopped and looked up. He said, "that's a joke." Everyone laughed gently.

"That's good, Pete. Really good," Hat replied. "I really like that." And he was off with his load, still chuckling."

## 7

"We talked about how magic mathematics was to Pythagoras and Aristotle and everyone in between and since." Jacob was walking along his timeline and tapping the names as he made his way back to the front of the room. "I'm barely giving you a glimpse of the centuries of study that justified their fascination. We have not escaped that attraction even today. Ever hear of POP?" He put the capitals on the board.

A couple of hands went up. "Sebastian?"

"It is whether it will rain or not. If it is over 50, we need our coats."

"Well done. Some people who study weather have figured out that when particular conditions exist, like high temperature and high humidity, all things they measure with instruments and attach numbers to, that there is a certain likelihood that it will rain or snow. And to make it easy for us to understand, they give it as a percentage. Fifty percent probability of precipitation," he tapped the letters as he said the words. It means that it is a coin flip. If the POP gets higher, then the odds are that it will rain or snow, when they say. So the fascination with numbers and how they could predict our life continues."

"Today's lesson gives us another reason to be amazed at numbers, and I'm using it to illustrate an important fundamental in logical thinking. All the people who studied circles eventually got around to wondering how big circles were inside the circumference. We call it the circle's area." Children were beginning to slump. Interest from thoughts of rain and outside were fading fast.

"We could do the same sort of studies that we did with the triangles and the circles to find that the area inside a circle, the number of tiles it would take to cover it," he drew a circle and hastily covered it with hatching. The sound of chalk and pattern of marks brought attention back for a moment. "Area was always related to its circumference. If one went up, so did the other in exactly the same proportion." More sighs.

"Hope is on the Horizon team. Two more minutes." The announcement brought puzzled looks.

"What's in two minutes," one whispered.

"Shhh." "Let me say this before everyone falls asleep," Jacob resumed. "Area is also related to the circle's diameter." He added that to the notes on the board. "Because both circumference and diameter were related to the circle's area, then diameter was related to circumference," He drew the connection to make a triangle.

"This got shortened up as follows, and this is what you have to memorize." Eyes came up.

"If A=B and B=C, then A=C." He drew a box around the syllogism and stood back personally satisfied but struggling to imagine how to make it relevant to the children who were writing studiously in their books.

Some had turned to creating more decorative boxes when he said, "OK, let's bring that into your world. Brian won't eat broccoli." He wrote it down. "No, don't write this," he directed as weary brains reached for pens. "This is a game."

He repeated the line, and then added, "Mom says Bryan must eat his broccoli before he gets dessert."

"So what's the conclusion?"

"Bryan doesn't get dessert."

"Bingo. He went back and drew the triangle that linked the thoughts. He scribbled in 'A=B' and 'B=C' below the starting statements and then, in colour, added 'A=C' below the conclusion.

"Let's try to make up some more syllogisms - that's what these triangular reasonings are called." There was confused muttering, so Jacob started.

"All birds lay eggs," he wrote, and then added, "Crows are birds." He could feel the expectation building as he finished writing on the board.

"So ...."

"Crows lay eggs," the class answered almost in unison.

They went on creating more. Most got sillier until Alisha said. "It isn't always true, though."

The laughing stopped. "Crows are black," she began. "My dog is black. So my dog is…"

Everyone burst out laughing.

"Without you in my classroom, this would not be nearly as much fun," Jacob laughed. "You make an excellent point that I hope all of you took note of. Be careful of the truths you start with and which you try to connect. Syllogisms can lead to new insight, but they can also reveal absurd connections - which can be another revealing discovery. Enough for today."

## 8

Jacob and TD had to step outside the bubble to talk; it was so noisy inside. "How're we doing?" Jacob asked.

"Outside cladding on both sides of all boxes, along with the roofs on each, will be done on time." The addition of a low-slope peaked roof along the length of each wouldn't be needed when in their final place in the tower, but it was aesthetically pleasing. If ever an owner wanted to leave and take his home with him, it would be needed in a stand-alone setting.

"It was a genius idea that Dan came up with to make the back of the boxes into the front. It will be a snap to insert the picture window. Fiddling about trying to turn the doors on the front of the box into a solid smooth wall to take a window was going to be a real pain in the--" He caught himself just in time.

"Anyways, we can finish the ends when we move outside. The boxes are good to go."

"Toilet units ready?"

"In place and being connected to the mains today. We're going to blitz the box moving overnight, so the floor should be clear a day ahead. They should be able to deflate over the weekend. We can hook up the units to the services any time."

"Is it just me, or has something changed? Maybe the laughing is what I notice. It's not loud like ridicule, but sort of like a chuckle 'round the bar."

"You're right. Working together has really bonded the guys. Everyone calls each other by name now. Haven't seen anyone drinking or drugging. Hell, they're all too busy. They seem to know where everyone is all the time. It all seemed to start after the fight, everyone was really p-- ticked off at... What was his name?"

"Zid?"

"Yeah. Anyways, that sort of reset the whole process. Those guys from the community college were great, also."

"That reminds me..." Jacob fished the folding military knife with the marlinspike from his pocket and handed it to TD.

"Shhh... I thought I'd lost this."

"Thank Hat."

They both stood silently looking at the weapon. "I'd have killed that guy, you know. When I heard that scream, I was--"

Jacob folded TD's fingers over the knife. "Put it away,

Daryl. Your buddies brought you back. It's over now." It disappeared into his pocket.

It took a moment to get his thoughts back on track. "Dan came up with another idea that isn't in the plans."

"Shoot."

"Don't say things like that to a soldier."

"Sorry."

"When the units go into their slots in the tower, we're going to be left with those four toilet units - twelve thrones each, as surplus. Dan's suggesting they could be hoisted to the top two floors under the dining room. There will be two for each floor to serve as washrooms for banquet centers. They would be an easy refit. Our own lounge and cafeteria will be on the top up there, but he's figured that we could turn the floors below into conference facilities, at least until there's the need to use those floors for housing. Could earn income, do jobs for some of the men, maybe be an entertainment venue."

"Where does this guy get these ideas? That's brilliant. Has he run this past the engineers?"

"Shall I say they are still recovering from the shock? Some street stray should not be imagining things like that apparently. You may pass the word. See how Ms. Lindsay responds."

"I was headed there now."

"OK. I should be back with my guys."

"I think we need a party in the place before they take it down. Friday night?"

"We'll all be there."

"Eight?"

"Done. Oh, and thanks." TD patted his pocket.

As he walked toward Lindsay Tower, Jacob thought he'd have to alert his class to the take-down so they could watch from the top floor patio.

9

"They look like Lego blocks," Anya said, looking down on the parking lot with the other children, each noting some new change as the covering deflated.

"It's going off to cover a soccer field," said Phillip.

Jacob was explaining the clustering to the teenagers. "Each unit backs up to the central toilet facility. They have their own bathrooms, of course, but it's too complicated to connect up all those units to the city system for less than a year. By the fall, these will be moving into the tower that will go up over there," he pointed to the distant end of the parking lot.

"So in the meantime, they built these units that have 12 separate toilet, shower and sink units. Attach them by a really short hallway, like six inches," he held out his hands to show. "That's what they're doing right now. Put in a short floor and secure it, then drop down these 'U' shaped pieces into the slot between the buildings to make a roof over the doorway, screw it in place on each side, and seal up the cracks with goop." They could hear the bzzzzt, sounds of power equipment driving home the screws.

"Who lives in those places?" Kyle asked.

"When they are ready, a bunch of men without homes will live there," Jacob explained. "The workers are actually the guys who are going to live in them. They're my friends. Some have lost their jobs, been injured; some have really difficult mental afflictions to deal with. In most cases, they just wander the streets. I met many during last summer. They were living under the bridge down the river?" Kyle and his friends nodded. They knew where the bridge was.

"Anyway, they did a big service for Ms. Lindsay that helped her realize a dream she'd had for a long time. Just as this is a place of shelter for you and your moms who had to escape really bad times, so those guys all have similar stories. They need help to escape from where they are to where they could be."

"My mom asked for a new apartment," David said. "She said she didn't want to look out to that tower full of men first thing every day. She's worried my dad will show up in it."

"I'm sorry to hear that," Jacob replied. "How about you?"

David shrugged. "Will she send me over there if I'm bad?"

Jacob drew David away from the group and crouched in front of the worried youth. "David, your mom had a terrible time before she got here. It hurt her a lot, and it's hard for her not to remember it. But you are the light of her life. She would never send you away. Never."

David looked down into Jacob's face. "She will never send you away, David." he repeated and hugged the child. David did not flinch. After a moment, Jacob set him back. "OK?"

David gave a weak smile and nod. "OK." He took the child's hand, and together they walked back to the group. "David," he said when they were at the railing, "I never asked you what you said to bring the secretary back to the classroom so fast that day.

"I did what you said." When Jacob looked blank, the boy went on. "I opened the door and screamed that you had dropped dead, and there was blood all over the place." She was on the telephone; she dropped it right on the desk and came right away.

"Remind me to tell you the story of "Crying Wolf."

"Do wolves cry?"

"I'll tell you another day. Look, they're starting to roll up the covering."

# 10

"When do we find out which place is our own?" Gary asked at the closing party in the empty cavern. The silence that followed indicated the interest.

Jacob was caught off-guard. "Weren't they all the same?" he thought. "I'd been so focused on getting them weather-tight that I hadn't thought about that. What do y'all think?"

Everyone was talking at once.

"We still got a lot of common tasks to complete - the same job on each unit. Doing the electrical, putting up drywall, installing plumbing."

"How about when it comes to doing the painting and putting in furniture? We're each going to want our own touch there. For now, it's just production line stuff."

That drew universal approval. The next question threatened to break it.

"Who gets to be where in the building? I want a penthouse with a south view."

There were a few sharp retorts, more laughs.

"Said he on the welfare cheque."

"Would you like the helipad option for your private plane as well?"

But the shuffling and the wrinkled brows said that it was a concern to all. They enjoyed working together and had built camaraderie amongst themselves that might be battered by someone getting special treatment. Instinctively they knew that was dangerous to their group, but nobody suggested how to fix the problem.

"Would placement in the building be okay for a lottery?" Jacob could feel the angst rising. His suggestion did not change it.

TD spotted a problem. "There'd be a black market in placement. As soon as places were allotted, someone could trade his off to someone who felt hard-done-by for money or something else. It plays into the hand of habits that will eat us up. Not good, guys." There was broad agreement.

"We could arm wrestle for places."

"As the one who would lose that, hands down," Dan said, holding up his partial hand. "Maybe this would help." Most chuckled at his dark humour. "I've been looking at the plans a lot, and there is something you might not know. Anybody got a wax marker?" A couple came out of overall pockets.

"Let me draw a plan of what each floor looks like. Back

up, guys." In a few minutes, he scribed out on the dirty floor a series of concentric circles and then began to explain.

"This is like taking the roof off and looking down on any floor. This circle in the middle is for the hoist that will bring each house up to whatever floor it's supposed to be on. It's like a railway roundhouse that can turn and slide the house into its slot. So every floor has a bunch of houses sticking out like petals on a daisy around this central service cylinder. Can you imagine them on the floor? There will be twelve on each floor and one extra open space without a house for the elevator access and whatnot." He started to scratch them off.

"Now, the back corners of each house almost touch, but there is about three feet on each side of the house at the other end. That's where the door is." The guys were muttering as they got the picture. "Between your neighbour and your door in the side at the front corner of your unit is about six or seven feet. You could put a chair there to chat if you both want. It's a bit wider than an apartment hallway. It fades back in a wedge shape to the back corner. Got it."

"So, out the front window of your unit is the promenade that is about twenty feet wide, and on the outside of that is the curtain wall of windows. Stairs or ramps link from one floor to another. Now think of this; your house is forty feet long, that promenade is half of that. That is a wide, wide hallway, man - two lanes of traffic! From your house, it is a lot of pavement and sky you'll see beyond that. Nobody is looking at the vista. If you want to see the poor people, you have to get out of your place and walk across the promenade - everybody will - and you can't tell anyone to get out of your view because it is a public thoroughfare." People began to nod and chuckle as they got the picture.

"The part about the penthouse view is that everybody will have it. In each apartment, there is a sixty-inch hi-res TV. You could put it on a side wall or across the front window, I suppose, but it comes with feed from the closed circuit cameras on the roof. The engineers were showing me that each of you could switch to whatever feed you want, from any side up there and it would look like you had the best suite in the place. The TVs will be framed like windows; you won't know they aren't. You could even turn on a fan to pretend you'd opened the window… Or you could take the elevator up to the top floor and look over the patio railing."

As the picture began to pass like a sunrise across the group, there were chuckles and new excitement. "Chr--" one began and caught himself. "I can't wait to get out of that rathole I'm in. If it means I can be in here next week, I'll put up all the God damned drywall myself."

"So I think it really boils down to trying to pick your floor neighbours. Are there some you want to be with, some who need your help? We all have to help each other to live, you know."

That turned the conversation around completely. People were already looking at others with raised eyebrows and nods or handshakes. Jacob was trying to spot those who hadn't spontaneously been invited into a cluster and drew them towards one.

In reporting it later to Maggie, he had trouble finding adequate words to describe the effect of Dan's intervention. Amazing just didn't cut it.

## 11

Maggie had listened to Jacob's description of the final party in the balloon even as she stared out the window of her office. Jacob was a bit disappointed that she didn't turn with bright eyes and smiles to respond to his excitement. When she did turn around, she was not close to smiling.

"You have solved an immediate and a mid-term problem, but there is another on the horizon that is life-threatening to the continuity of the community you are trying to build. Sooner or later, it will need to be addressed." Her tone and the way she leaned across the desk said she was about to do so.

"You are creating great buddy systems that will culture memorable stories till the cows come home. You will have filled four floors of the twenty with a ghetto designed to keep others out. It is not supposed to be a modern monastery." Jacob was shocked at the analysis.

"You know the arithmetic as well as I do. The bottom four floors are for services and professional rentals that offer employment to the men, and I'm not including the two sub-basements for parking. You've filled four floors with the first cohort of homeless men. The top one is going to be the lounge and cafeteria. It still leaves eleven floors in the twenty, for people yet to arrive." Jacob still couldn't see the problem.

"So how do you integrate those new arrivals that are just as needy into the community, so that community continues? You'll have to break up your nice little neighbourhoods to let newbies in or seed the new floors with alumni clumps to train the initiates. You have created a culture based on the possession of a home. It caters to the desire for permanence. Those guys may not want to move out or even move around within the building. You are building new divisions to replace those that you are trying to escape from. Have you wondered if you are seducing weak people with what they are most vulnerable to?" As the idea took root, Jacob began to have a bad feeling. He'd not been looking beyond the immediate.

"Well, one of the thoughts that came up a while ago is that we could devote one of the floors, maybe two, to a theatre and convention site. The engineers were looking at the structural needs and saw no problems. We suggested that the toilet trailers fitted for a dozen habitats on the ground could be hoisted into place on two floors and retrofitted without problems. TD suggested that a theatre sometimes needs a set-building workshop. Maybe we could build sets for off-site productions. That could be the way to connect new workers with old and then the housing could follow."

"Sounds like wishful thinking, Jacob. You need to think about this problem because it is coming at you. You need to do some cost-benefit planning as well as the social thing if this is to last more than a decade. If you don't solve it, this will not be a rescue haven for current and coming generations of homeless men; it will become an old men's home. That was not the purpose." The edge in Maggie's summary was not subtle.

"Got it," he sighed. He got up without preamble and headed for the door. He noted the dint left from when she had hurled whatever it was at him a year ago, the time he had brought the alarming information about her lover. A coat hook had been screwed into the space, and it almost covered the blemish. The table beside the door where he had put the telephone number was still there.

He closed the door quietly.

## 12

The pitch at dinner in Lindsay Tower with the moms had paid off. He'd pointed out how university or college might not be on the horizon for some of their children. He knew not to tell a mother her child wasn't smart enough, so he avoided that. It was the economic argument that had many nodding. "If your child wants to be an apprentice, they'll pay him or her while they are in training. They graduate with a job. It isn't the university path where you might graduate in debt for decades and without good job prospects," he's said. The clincher, he thought, was the oblique reference to automation. "There is hope for robots to take over the jobs in the trades in the near future. Everything breaks down, and it takes a human to make the fixes."

"And it will give your children an appreciation for the construction trades," he'd added because it was on his list of points. He'd come away with permission for the class to visit the men who were building their homes down below.

TD was to be their guide. Jacob made sure he was beside Alisha when they were invited into one that was completed. Her mom had said that it was in one of those that they had escaped their homeland. Her brother died before the container arrived, where it let them out. She was only an infant, but she might remember.

"I'm starting with one that has had its paint put on yesterday. The bed will be added as soon as we're out of here. It hangs from the ceiling so the man can work underneath. He does a lot of bodybuilding with weights and stuff. When the bed goes up, there is his gear, and when he goes to sleep, the bed hides it."

"The bathroom is not hooked up till we get into the tower. For now, the private toilet and shower are in the unit next door - through that doorway." He pointed. "The living space is about the size of two big bedrooms - about 300 square feet. You can convert that to square meters if you want."

"Now we're going to go back in time to see the way this was a few days ago." He led them down the row to a noisy unit.

"Give me minute, guys," he called. "We have our first visitors." Welcomes were called as tools went down. It felt crowded when the children squeezed in. "The sides are corrugated, and in those wiggles, we put wooden boards called studs. We lay them in flat so they only stick up the width of my thumb. Later we foam insulation between the studs. You can see in this cross wall to separate the bathroom the holes where we string the wires. Show them how you do that, Thumb." The man threaded a white cable through holes at hip height and pulled. The spool beside one child rattled and startled him.

"These wires bring electricity to the receptacle boxes from the panel back here." He pointed to a breaker box. "Each run goes to a separate circuit breaker so you can make repairs, if you need to, to one circuit without turning everything off. He picked one circuit breaker out of the box to show how the switch flipped. "They are colour coded for the amount of electricity they can carry." He pointed to a red one.

"Why do they call you Thumb?" asked Leiah.

"Used to do a lot of hitchhiking, and to ask for a ride, you stick out your thumb." He stuck out his curved thumb from huge hands. "Can you do that?"

Leiah stuck out a stubby thumb.

"Your thumb is curved."

"I must have used it a lot, and many people passed me by. I guess the wind from all those cars just blew it into a curve."

Leiah looked at her thumb all the way to the next stop.

The last stop had no interior work at all. It was dark beyond the work light that pushed at the shadows. It was rusty and smelled odd. Jacob was in mid-group with Alisha. She took two steps into the grubby space and froze. "Something is wrong. I don't feel well." Jacob pulled her aside for the others to pass, and then turned her gently.

"We'll wait outside."

As they stood listening to TD's description from a distance, Jacob pointed out that the corrugated sides that you could see inside were covered by insulation and siding on the outside. "We wanted them to look like houses or trailers - anything but a box. That's why they have those decorative roofs."

"Why did I feel suddenly sick?"

"Well, it did smell funny. Maybe it reminded you of something you didn't like? Are you feeling better now? Take a few more big breaths. Here they come." The class dawdled out.

"Each of the homes will go into the tower when it is ready." He pointed to the steelwork rising rapidly at the other end of the parking area. Then, he illustrated how the homes would be pulled on flatbeds into the middle of the building and set on an elevator that could rotate like the crane was doing with lots of hand motions and sound effects. "The elevator goes up the floor where the house should be, and the box is pulled into its slot. So there will be twelve on each floor, all pointed out like petals on a flower. Here, like this one." He picked up a daisy growing through a crack.

They were on their way back to the classroom after suitably thanking TD and waving at each of the guys working in the other units as they passed when Kyle said, "Sounds like modern-day Diogenes. They'll be living in boxes because they can't find barrels. What they got are barrels with curtains."

13

The rate at which the building was climbing into the sky was astonishing to Jacob. Steel girders were swinging into place every time he looked out the window. Every night the convoy of flatbeds carrying pre-formed concrete floor slabs arrived like clockwork. By the following morning, the building was another floor higher.

"We really need to get the solar collector in place as soon as we can. If we don't, you guys are going to be cold next spring when the heat runs out," the engineer had explained as they watched the ceramic container for the molten salt storage being built in place.

He was as good as his word. By month's end, the building was topped off, and they were assembling the array of mirrors on the ground ready to be lifted to the roof and secured around the spherical collector. Asa, the stationary engineer from Lindsay Tower, came over to run tests on pumps and heat exchangers before going live.

The curtain wall of windows had not kept pace with the floor building, but even so, the lower levels were now enclosed, and the word had gone out to the guys on house construction that they'd be needed to start installing interior walls in the tower for the professional suites as soon as possible - yesterday would be fine.

The timetable raised some hackles amongst the former vagrants. Some had learned how to put in time too well for the contractor who would pay a steep financial cost for not making the milestones in the contract. If the walls weren't in place, the wiring and plumbing couldn't be finished.

"So move your asses," one of the foremen shouted.

It burned him when one team held up a finger and tut-tutted him. "No more naughty language now. You know the rule." The foreman's red-faced reaction was worth it.

Dan had them ahead of schedule by laying outlines with a wax marker on the floor for the walls once he'd confirmed them with the engineer. It was the way they'd worked out in the home building. The guys worked well under appropriate direction.

The stud team, who bragged about their name, were first on scene-setting floor plates. The first was hardly set before the verticals, and top plate was being raised. Not to be outdone, the power team was hassling the Studs to pick up the pace so they could run the wiring. It was all good-natured and wonderfully effective. After they passed, the dry-wallers, still working in the houses, would be coming in.

Pete had gone off on his morning rounds of the

houses that were still being finished to collect up cutoffs, wire spools, scraps, the detritus of a construction site, but he hadn't returned. For someone who was punctual to a fault, it was peculiar. TD headed off on Pete's route to find him.

"By here a while ago. Brought us some wire and duplex receptacles. You know you'd think that guy was telepathic," reported Gary at his first stop.

"Said he'd bring us a couple of gas cylinders," said Thumb, who was doing plumbing for the showers. "He was headed toward stores."

That is where TD found him, leaning on his cart and rocking his head back and forth, moaning.

"Over here, man," TD said as he drew him out of traffic to sit on a stack of pallets. Pete wouldn't look up.

"What's wrong, soldier?"

"Shouldn't be here."

"The guys said you were getting stuff for them. You're supposed to be here. You were carrying out your assignment. That's what reliable people do."

"Him."

"Who?"

"The guy."

There was only one person; TD could imagine that Pete would call by that name. He knew everyone by name and had been making significant progress in using them.

"Stay here."

While TD was signing for a couple of small tanks of propane for the plumbing torch, he scanned the list of people who had picked up the material. There it was. Austin Zid, the guy who had set Pete off and who TD would have killed had he not dropped his knife. "Who's this guy Zid?" he asked.

The store's master shrugged. "Doin' electrical in the parking area of the tower. He was just here. Needed a box of conduit clips."

"Thought he was kicked off the site?"

"Don't know about that."

Pete was where he'd left him, but he wasn't rocking. TD handed the cylinders to him. "Gary said he needs these."

"No, it was Thumb," Pete corrected quietly.

"Let's find him, then Bruce."

While Bruce was talking to Pete, TD spotted the site supervisor and hustled to catch up with him.

"There is a restraining order against one of the electricians - Austin Zid. He's been banned from the site, but he just signed out material from stores."

The supervisor blew out a big breath then looked up. "The order applies to the container conversion site, not the tower. He is top of the union list, so I'm obliged to hire him. If I send him off, the whole union will be on my case. I can't take a shutdown with the timelines we've got. Sorry. He's within the law, and he's done nothing wrong on this side of the fence."

"He terrified one of my men - beaten him."

"I heard it was you who did the beating, but I can't do anything. Suggest you keep the other guy away." He pulled out a cell phone to answer a call. "Be right there." He turned back to TD. "I guess you could lodge a complaint, but I can tell you how it will end. He's not on your site, and he's done nothing wrong. Gotta go."

"When Pete starts working with the guys in the tower, he could come across this guy again," TD said to Bruce.

Bruce stared down. "Well, I gave him a sedative. That'll work, but if he's going to be even close to that guy, maybe we should do some desensitizing training instead of loading the kid up with drugs."

They arranged to meet and watch from a distance as the workers ate their lunches. TD took them up onto the second floor, where some of the guys were putting up interior walls with Dan. They could look down on the lunch tables.

"We're just getting used to seeing him, Pete," Bruce said. "What shut you down was the surprise. We're trying to take away the surprise."

Pete stared down at the men silently. When lunch was over, and the men got up, Pete said, "He took the wrong cooler."

"No, he's got the one he came in with," Bruce corrected. He looked back at the blue and white cooler with the bale handle that was swinging at Zid's side as he left the lunch area.

Pete just shook his head.

"Well, let's meet here tomorrow, and we'll do a bit more desensitizing. See me after you check-in if you need more meds, eh?"

"OK," Pete said with resignation.

For the rest of the week, Pete met with Bruce and TD, and they watched from their spot. Each time, Zid left with a different lunch cooler than the one he'd brought - identical but definitely not the same one. The one he picked up was brought in by one of the carpenters one time when that worker sat beside him for lunch. Another time it was a steelworker. Each time, the two men would sit down, exchange pleasantries then open their coolers for the food inside. After eating, Zid would pull over the other worker's cooler and set his own lid on it, get up and walk off and leave it by the gate where he could pick it up as he left the site for the day.

In the week following, Bruce would walk with Pete past the lunch area when Zid was there. They walked behind the man, so they were not seen. It was close enough to get Pete used to any normal situation in the workplace. He could even use the man's name without choking up. When Bruce was reporting Pete's progress back to TD, both men were stunned to hear Pete's addition to the conversation.

"The drinks in his cooler aren't cold," Pete said.

"How do you know that?"

"They aren't wet on the outside. Everyone else has wet drinks."

TD looked at Bruce and asked, "Why do you suppose he carried a cooler that doesn't cool?"

The next day, while Bruce and Pete did their walk-by, TD took pictures to show Pete how close he'd gotten to his adversary... And what the shared coolers looked like.

*

TD led the Dry Walling team, in freshly scrubbed

overalls, to work in the tower on Monday. There were twenty of them. "Can we take our lunch pails up on the floor? The men have their water in them."

"No problem."

He made sure the men took their lunch after seeing Zid get up and leave his lunch box at the gate. When his men had finished, so did they. The lineup of twenty-five identical coolers was pretty impressive. TD made sure the ones that had been there were moved in the process. Each of his team could identify their own by the notches cut into the underside of the handle when their names wouldn't do.

Many didn't want to put their names on their boxes. "People can put stuff in your box if they have a grudge or something. If they don't see your name, they don't know which is yours," they agreed. A life of challenging experience left its scars.

"There was some good-natured banter as the men got their lunch containers and lined up to exit. "I think this is yours," TD said to Winston as he slid it towards him with his toe, knowing full well it was not. "This is mine."

The truck delivering steel interrupted the flow out of the gate. TD saw that Zid was stuck far back.

"Good to see you, Jacob," TD hailed as he and Winston walked through the gate. They strode across the street to the group dressed in leather windbreakers and jeans. As requested, Jacob had Pete with him and Detective Winters from the local police force. Jacob had earned a card with the detective's personal number after saving the kid from the suicide vest last fall and then snaring the con artist that almost got away with the fortune of Ms. Lindsay, who ran the shelter for abused women.

There was handshaking and greetings as the men jostled. "Could we go for a brew?" TD asked. In the back and forth of the discussion that followed, TD snuck a peek and saw Zid's back as he walked towards the parking area, a blue and white insulated lunch container swinging carelessly by his side.

When he turned back, TD was stone-faced. "Detective, you saw me pick up my lunch bucket on the other side of that fence, did you not?"

"Yeah." Winters was not smiling anymore.

"And Winston also?"

Another nod.

"We need to hand these over to you in a secure way, so there is no doubt later on. Can we go to that pub down the street to make the transfer? Maybe you could call up a buddy as a witness." Together, the group made its way to the patio. Winters was talking on his phone as they dodged pedestrians who shared the street.

"Pete, tell the detective who this cooler belongs to."

"It's the one Mr. Zid left after lunch at the gate."

"How do you know that?"

"The label," Pete said, pointing to the remnant that a thumbprint could cover. "TD's has a square label; Zid's has a corner missing. It looks like a sideways checkmark." TD turned the box to show the torn label on the lid.

"The one I took to work also has four notches cut on the underside of the handle. This isn't it. I must have picked up the wrong one by mistake."

Winter's eyes came up. He knew a switch when he saw it. He looked past TD to see a comrade in plain clothes.

"So I need you to open this lunch box."

"Will it explode?"

"Hope not."

Winters signed for the new officer to lift the lid. "A couple of empty water bottles and a freezer gel pack," he reported.

TD sat back in surprise but then picked up a serviette from the table and gave it to the officer. "Pick up the gel pack."

The man reached around the crushed plastic bottles to grab the gel pack. As soon as he did, his face changed. "It's not soft. It's hard. There is something inside it."

The officer tipped the plastic bag onto a new serviette, and a packet of bills slid into his hand. Jacob noticed the colour first - brownish - and the value in the corner - 100. "Are those all hundred dollar bills?" he gasped.

The policeman spread them like he was spreading a deck of cards. They were. And on all he saw, there was an inky note right near the dollar value. Each seemed to carry a three-number addition. The numbers disappeared from view when the bills slid back into the package.

"Please put it back and open this one," TD said as he handed over the second cooler. "This is the one that one of the steelworkers brought in, and that was supposed to go home with him," TD explained. He elaborated on how Zid did the switching of the bottom sections of the containers.

"Just a gel pack." The officer said as he looked in. "It is filled with... ...feels like small packages." He hastily put them back into the cooler as the waiter approached.

"Can I get you guys something to drink?"

"We were all going to have an ale, but Jake here just reminded us we were supposed to be celebrating with a friend. Could you bring me the lunch buckets I left here last night? The bartender said he'd leave them behind the bar at the end."

When he'd gone, TD said. "I think there is something bad going on at the construction site, and you have the evidence. I know we can leave it in your capable hands."

"How do we know you didn't just set someone up?"

"Well, I guess you can check my fingerprints against any you find inside. So maybe we should do that now, or should we wait till the morning?"

The young waiter returned with two more white and blue lunch coolers looking just like the two at the policeman's feet.

"There was a sale," TD explained.

He gave one to Winston and took the other new one for himself. "I guess you can handle those," he said to the police. "If you wanted to blow your cover, you could keep them, or maybe you could just leave them back at the site once you've checked them out."

They all scraped to their feet. TD handed the waiter a twenty-dollar bill. "Thanks. Sorry that we can't stay." To the others, he asked, "Shall we go?"

14

Zid was back at the construction site just before midnight, and he was in a lather. The security guard made him wait while he did the paperwork for the floor panels on the flatbed in front of him.

"OK, what's your problem?" he shouted as the diesel snarled into gear and followed the one ahead into the unloading area.

"I picked up the wrong lunch bucket," Zid held out the one he had. "It looked like this one."

"What is it with lunch buckets? Two of the new guys were griping about the same thing. Somebody stole my lunch bucket," he whined in parody. "No bloody surprise. I think they all got the same kind. Looked like an end display at a hardware store. I told them to sort it out tomorrow. But there are two still over there against the fence." Zid could see what the truck had previously obscured. A new truck was pulling through the gate with the next load of floor panels. "Now, get out of my way. I'm busy."

Zid dodged around the truck as it stopped. He

yanked off the tops of both and searched in the dark bottoms. Whew! He could tell just by feeling that they were his and the steelworker's. He set the one he'd brought down and picked up both; he'd searched and headed back to his car on the run.

The truck had pulled ahead into the queue when the Security Guard looked up as new headlights swept the space. Only one of the lunch coolers lay where the two had been. "Guess it was his," he thought. "But wait, didn't he bring one also. Maybe he brought two - big eater or something. Some guys did. Didn't matter anyway; not my job." The next truck was edging up to the gate. He hit the switch to open it.

\*

"Five thousand, six hundred dollars in hundred dollar bills, were retrieved from a gel pack bag that had been emptied and repurposed to hold the money. It opened at the left end when the title was face up. It was marked in secrecy as follows..." the report read.

"Of the fifty-six bills, thirty-eight had three-digit numbers added in pencil or pen in the margin. The bills were stacked in order according to these numbers. The numbers are listed on the attached sheet in numerical order as they were found starting at the top (face side up)."

"Photographs were taken (see attached). Standard protocols were used to conclude the bills were not counterfeit. Initial analysis of the numbers suggested they had probably been written by one person, no more than a few, definitely not by many people. Photographs have been sent for further analysis to--" Winters knew the expert.

"In the plastic pack in the second cooler, now also marked with our identification code below, were eighteen plastic, zip-locked packages of white powder. Samples were taken from each and sent for analysis, and the packages were micro-dotted as follows…"

Winters slid his finger back along the page, then up. "Eighteen packages, thirty-eight bills and thirty-eight were marked with numbers, so there were…" he jotted the numbers on the corner of the report and did the subtraction long-hand, "…eighteen un-numbered bills and eighteen packets of… probably sugar or baking soda," he thought wryly. "Sounds a bit coincidental. Wonder why the thirty-eight were numbered?" He mentally stacked the bills in two piles. "Ha. There are two operations going on and one collector. Wonder what the other one is?"

## 15

Jacob and the children were watching as the mirrors were hoisted into position around the collector's vessel on the new tower across the parking lot. Asa, their stationary engineer who operated the one on their own building, was doing the play-by-play commentary.

"The sphere in the middle will have sunlight focused on it, and when that happens, it will be scalding," she explained. "We'll pipe special coolants into it to pick up the heat and carry it down to the storage space in the ground there behind the line of portable toilets. That heat is what will heat the building next winter. It is why we had to get things going fast."

"Watch, here comes another mirror." The construction crane lifted the shrouded package from the flatbed that had moved the unit from the assembly area to the foot of the tower. "The mirrors had to be covered for transit and storage till we could place them because if a mirror wasn't covered, and the truck stopped for a traffic light, and if the sun was in the right spot, the mirror could focus the light on something besides the road and set it on fire. Imagine a whole string of burning houses along the street at every traffic light."

The children burst into chatter and hand-waving as a death ray was imagined and portrayed with an explosive passion.

"Here it comes," Asa continued. "It is going to be dropped into its hanger that is computer powered, to keep it focused on the collector even as the sun moves. We'll leave the cover on until the crane is taken down. We don't want anybody in the way when we start to focus on those mirrors. You can see that there are already six mirrors in their cradles." Some counted the blue-wrapped blobs.

Jacob let his eyes drift down to where window units were being installed to enclose the floor a few levels below. The panels came up on the internal hoist that would later move the men's houses up. They'd come to the floor and be off-loaded by a front end loader which would then carry the unit that was about thirty feet long and contained five windows. It needed a skilled driver to swing the panel into alignment with the outer edge of the floor on which it was to be secured, and then slowly move it out to its exact placement. There was only a fraction of an inch clearance top and bottom.

The men required to fasten the windows were well aware of the need to stand clear while the window panel was moved into place and keep their tethers untangled. But the harnesses still needed to be loose enough to allow them to move about to reach the brackets and bolt them home. The panels aligned with preset fittings in the floor and ceiling. As Jacob watched, his eyes shot open, and his voice stuck in his throat. It was the child beside him who screamed.

The panel moving into place had just swept a worker right off the floor and out the space where the window was to go. The man flew into the air as though he'd been launched from a springboard. His arms were waving for anything to grab. He was screaming. The sound was time-delayed by the distance, only arrived as the child who was pointing through the canyon of air between them squealed, "He fell!" The scream was followed by an immediate crash as the man swung back against the building.

As she said it, the puppet of a person jerked to a halt, dangling in front of the windows two floors below where he'd been working. It was plain he was hanging by his harness, and he was upright, but his yellow hardhat arched silently to the ground. His orange tether swung the man back and forth until he managed to get turned around and his feet against the building. The distant shouting conveyed the panic and response that Jacob imagined must have erupted on the floor.

Jacob watched as the window panel that had been oblique retreated into the cavity of the floor, and now three workers, tightly secured and leaning out over the edge, were obviously doing what they needed to rescue the fallen man. Shouts were exchanged; another tether soared out to land beside the hanging worker who seemed to be trying to work his foot into a loop. That was when Jacob noticed that the man was not using his one arm, the one that had taken the impact as he crashed back against the building. In the next few minutes, the man was hoisted foot by foot up to the lip and then hauled out of sight and into the shadows.

*

Bruce did morning rounds, now that all those who had been on the street were in their own homes. Everyone was engaged in the tower construction as part of the plan to create a community with a standard and supportive purpose. He went along the row and banged on the doors of those who he knew had trouble getting up early. If they didn't show up at the breakfast tent, he was back at their door. It was the way he was keeping everybody on any medication they were taking and monitoring general health. Some of the guys had racked up pretty complicated health issues.

With regular meals and monitored intake, Bruce had been pleased to show how the people with diabetes were managing better, those with cholesterol were seeing decreases, and the usage of blood pressure medication was dropping. Nobody had relapsed back into the drug addictions that had beset them. Best of all, the men were happy, and every day he was cataloguing moments when they helped each other. They were opening up, privately and only occasionally, about family and bad times in the past.

Jacob listened to Bruce's summary attentively as they walked the shared route to the construction site and his classroom. It sounded awfully optimistic and awoke almost a reflexive caution in him... Maybe it was the time to get the thought his boss had dropped on him into someone else's head. "Ms. Maggie is saying what we're building here is an old men's home. They guys are getting so bonded to each other there will be no room for anyone else to come in, nor will any want to leave. It is not the corporate objective."

Bruce drew a breath. "Well, not to disparage the lady's world view, she doesn't know her a--" he was about to go on more colourfully but caught himself. "What she sees is the success of treating people properly. It's only a step on the way. Do I expect to minister to these guys for the rest of my life? Hardly. And it is the same for them all. This is a step, the first one these guys have taken in a long time that didn't bite them back. And as soon as the men can see past dinner, they will be out of here so fast; you'll be importing people to fill the place." He had gotten a little flushed, he realized and then stopped. He took a couple more breaths.

"Next time you see the lady, let her know that her concern is appreciated and is being taken under advisement." Jacob chuckled.

"Thanks for your eloquent and concise summary," Jacob replied. "It's my conclusion too, but I didn't know how to put it so well. I wanted to tell her to MYOB, but she's my boss. The last time I spoke truth to power, she threw an ashtray at me, and then before that, it got me kicked out of my job as spiritual leader."

"Welcome to the club," Bruce said as they parted each to their respective jobs.

\*

The biggest challenge some men had was deciding how to spend the leftover money not spent on housing and meals. There was a lot of talk after the evening meals about how to keep from gambling or boozing away the bundle that was building in their credit union accounts. Drugs were all too accessible when you knew where to get them. That night the financial advisers showed up to make a presentation was one Jacob laughed at still.

The men had invited representatives from two banks and the local credit union. The wealth managers from the banks showed up in suits and made presentations appropriate to a board room. The credit union guy appeared in dress slacks and a plaid shirt. It took him no time to tick off the charges that banks made for transfers, withdrawals, and every other service and the alternatives the credit union offered. He was called back the next week and had to bring help to sign up all the new accounts and switch others from banks.

But there was no avoiding the seduction of the casino model to wealth offered by lottery cards. It was talked about often both during the day on the building site and at mealtime. Jacob brought in a big card that initially looked like a cheque until you read it.

## Odds of scoring a big win in the lottery
# 1 in 13,983,816

He continued with the follow-up on the back of the card with the odds of being hit by lightning. About one-in-a-million here. 1 in 1,222,000 in the US. 1 in 15,300 if you live to be 80 in the US.

"Well, why do all those guys doing steel and in the other trades keep shelling out a hundred bucks pay for tickets. I heard one of them say the money was used to buy lottery tickets," Harold chipped in.

TD's eyes snapped up. "Say again?"

"That guy you clocked when he pushed Pete around; I saw him collecting C notes from all the workers the other day. The steelworker, don't know his name, but he said it was a lottery they were paying into."

"Sounds like a lot for a lottery ticket. Aren't they a couple of bucks each? And wouldn't they be buying new tickets each week, not once a month?"

"I've heard other groups pitch into a pot and use it to buy some tickets. Even heard of one bunch working in a warehouse who won a couple million once."

"Tell me about that again, Harold. Did just a few pay?"

"I saw everyone hand him a hundred dollar bill, and I think he wrote their name on it. Nobody gave him twenties. I'm pretty sure every man on the floor handed over a hundred bucks." He was about to go on but seemed to think better of it. TD wasn't listening anyway.

"Jake," TD muttered sideways to Jacob. "Can you give Winters a call? Ask him if there were names on money in those coolers. Even if he won't tell you, tell him what Harold just said."

*

Harold had another problem, maybe more. Bruce picked up on it when Harold slipped out the door instead of opening it wide as he used to when he'd first moved in. Bruce had had to come back to get him when Harold didn't show for breakfast. He'd hammered repeatedly and shouted he wasn't going without him. Eventually, he elicited a muffled and colourful epithet to accompany his request for a minute. They'd made it partway to the gate when Harold stopped and started taking deep breaths.

Bruce couldn't help slipping into diagnostic mode. "Unshaven, but good colour. Downed the bacon & egg on bread he'd brought and was working on the coffee. The pace was good, no stumbles. Avoided looking at me since he came out. Monosyllable answers."

"Want to tell me?"

"Zid and his buddies came on to me last night before I left. They wanted to be sure I knew about the accident. It seems the guy who was knocked off the floor was someone who had not paid up. Unless I contribute to the monthly lottery ticket fund, I might find something falls on me."

"You didn't say that when you were talking to TD."

"Hey, man. All I have to do is pay up, and it goes away. Do you know what TD will do if he finds out? Christ, he'd kill the bugger."

"Anybody else approached that you know?"

"Not that I heard."

"I want you to stay with me today." He could see TD in the lineup ahead and hailed him.

"I want Harold to work with me till I'm sure the new meds he is on don't give him a problem," he said as he drew TD out of the lineup so they could have a word in confidence. "Have you heard Zid is running an extortion game?"

"Tell me."

He did.

"Third guy they buttonholed that I know about. I told the dry wallers that they only work with our own and passed that on to the supervisor. We have enough men; he doesn't need to send anyone else. Pete has an escort to travel.

"Bruce shook his head. "This is bad."

TD shuffled a bit and pulled out his cell phone. From the case, he slid a folded hundred-dollar bill out of a pocket. "Tell Harold to give Zid this when Zid hits him up at lunch. Make a point of talking to some of the other guys, so Harold is alone for a few minutes. Tell him not to worry; we'll all be handy. Just tell him we need him to set the trap. The bill's been marked. We need to collect some information before we do anything about this."

Bruce had turned back to where Harold was waiting when TD called out. "Oh, and tell our guys that they are moving the port-a-potties after lunch. They'll be inside on the first floor. They have to move them so they can backfill around the foundations of the heat storage space."

Bruce handed over the bill to Harold as soon as they could make the exchange out of sight. "TD seems to have some sort of plan to trap Zid. He thinks that Zid will demand money at lunch and you're to give him this. It's been marked. I'll be over-talking to some of the others, but I'll only be steps away. He needs you to pass this over."

Harold nodded and tucked the bill into his breast pocket, and re-buttoned it.

Sure enough, Zid set his lunch bucket at the other end of Harold's table as soon as Harold sat down and Bruce stepped over to talk to Eustache. Zid never saw TD change the sandwiches in his lunch while he was zeroing in on his victim.

"Want to buy into the Lottery ticket co-op?" Zid leered as he approached.

Harold did not look up, only opened his pocket and held up the folded bill.

"Good man. Hope we're lucky this time." He leaned close to squint at Harold's site identification badge then wrote something on the bill before it went into his own pocket.

As Bruce approached, Zid backed off, still smirking. His buddies were gathering at the other end of the table and already had food opened. The smells wafted down the table. Bruce and Harold moved away, followed by laughs at some shared joke.

TD was watching from across the lunch area when Zid got up, saying he needed to take a crap. He picked up his lunch bucket and walked away. TD tapped Pete, and together they headed off to leave their buckets at the gate as well. Zid was hurrying by then. He seemed to have a sudden need for that toilet.

"Bring your cart," TD directed Pete urgently as they passed it. "Get the shovel driver to help you move those pallets onto it." He pointed to the half dozen that must have fallen off a truck across from the line of portable toilets. "Get him looking the other way."

Aside from the man waiting with his digger to move dirt, there was a truck about to move the line of portable toilets. Already, the service guy was hooking his hoist to the most distant toilet for lifting up onto the truck bed. He'd seen Zid go into the bathroom on the other end of the line and waved acknowledgement that he wouldn't move it till he was out. TD, with Pete in tow, headed to that other end of the line. TD saw Zid had just ducked into the bathroom.

TD and Pete picked up some scraps as they headed toward the pile of pallets. Just before they got there, TD made as though to go to the second bathroom from the end and waved at the excavator driver waiting for the bathrooms to be removed so he could do the backfilling. TD motioned and pointed to the pile and Pete. Pete was making a good try to lift one. TD held out beseeching hands. The driver came out of the cab. TD moved to the second toilet and, once out of sight, ducked immediately behind the first. Zid's groans had stopped, and the shuffling suggested hc was pulling up his pants.

The door opened, and Zid squinted as he stepped into bright light and spotted that wimp that picked up scraps. He didn't see the chunk of concrete that smashed into the side of his head. He was passed feeling dizzy as he was rolled over the embankment. He never felt the crush of dirt that fell on him a while later.

"Thanks for the help," TD said, hitching his pants and checking his fly. The machine driver nodded as they hoisted the last of the pallets onto Pete's cart.

\*

Everybody had figured out their own way to mark their lunch containers. Some left it by a particular post, and others put a rock on theirs. A few even resorted to their names. There was the usual good-natured joking about who had whose, the inevitable lid removal to prove they were right and the weary waves as people headed home. It had become almost a ritual.

When Pete bent down to pick up the cooler TD had just searched, removed a freezer pack, and closed, TD told him to leave it. "As a note," he said.

When the day shift had left, there was still one lunch cooler left along the fence. It had a torn yellow sticker on the lid, but it was empty, the security guard found. There was also one person who had not checked out. He reported the absence, and his supervisor investigated.

Austin Zid was last seen running to the bathroom after lunch. His tablemates said he'd not been feeling well after eating his chicken sandwiches.

The serviceman who had been moving the toilets confirmed the groans were coming from the bathroom he was about to move, suggesting someone was in distress. He'd started to remove the units at the other end of the line. The new ones he'd brought were already in place inside the building as required. There was nobody in the unit when he lifted it onto his truck. He hadn't seen the guy leave but thought he might have gone home. He sure moved and sounded like he had some sort of gastric distress.

The excavator operator confirmed that he'd helped Pete move pallets when TD went into the toilet for a wiz, and that TD had joined them to get the pallets onto Pete's cart that already had some short scraps on it. He'd started to backfill the trench as soon as the portable potty truck was out of the way and was finished on time. He'd seen someone go into the toilet while he was waiting before TD did, but he was busy helping Pete later. The guy could have easily left without him seeing. And he watched the service guy check that the toilet was empty before he hoisted it out.

So that left the supervisor to conclude that Austin Zid had left mid-afternoon before his shift ended in medical distress and hadn't checked out because he was ill and/or the guard on duty was busy with other traffic and tasks. It was no surprise then to see that Zid had not reported for work that morning. He probably had food poisoning from the sandwiches he ate. It always took a few days to get over that.

16

Harold hardly seemed changed even after the news got around that Austin Zid had gone home with tummy palaver and had not been back to work since. He'd also forgotten his lunch box. It was still at the gate, getting covered with deeper dust as the days went on.

Bruce continued to call for him each morning to walk over to the worksite. Harold still failed to show up for breakfast and edged through the door as though he kept a cat inside. Bruce brought him food-to-go along with his lunch in his cooler. He eventually decided he needed to ask Harold directly. "Hey man, are you starting to collect things again?"

Harold stopped, and his head jerked up, eyes wide like he'd been caught in a spotlight. "Ahhh... Ahhh... Not really. I've just been saving the papers to read after work."

"You been storing up clothes too? You know winter's coming." Harold took the enquiry as encouragement.

"Yeah, I found a thick coat with matching snow pants. Could sleep in a snowdrift with that gear."

"What did you do with your old one?"

"Well, it's still good. I'll save it for doing dirty work, you know." They walked on a few steps.

"Harold, you know that you can't keep doing that. You only start collecting stuff when something's eating at you. They aren't going to hoist your junk-filled house up to the floor you'll be on. There are load limits on the lift. We need to get those anxieties under control and the house cleaned up." The gate to the construction site was coming up. "Hey, let's skip work today. Let's go for a walk down along the river. We already got our lunches; we'll take over Jake's old table and solve the world's problems."

Harold didn't say anything.

Bruce knew he was pressing the man and maybe stepping over the line, but Harold was only going one way if he didn't do anything. "And I got some excellent weed. That might help, eh?"

Harold's eyes came up at the last suggestion.

"I have it for medicinal purposes - it's not street. I'm not becoming your local supplier."

While the promise still hung in the air, Bruce waved at the security guard and pointed to both himself and Harold and then did a slash across his throat. Security got the message and made a note on the entry list.

Bruce turned his patient away from the gate. The house call would be later.

\*

After dinner, Jacob was talking to Winston - "No, it was supper," Winston insisted - in the communal tent that served as their dining facility. "Dinner is a noon meal. You seem to have something missing in your childhood that you can't remember that," Winston kept joking. And he was right. It must be a carryover from childhood.

"Can we talk about how things are going? Ah, there's TD." They waved him over.

"TD joined them with his empty mug. "Good Dinner, eh?"

Winston threw up his hands.

Jacob nodded and turned to the troubled Winston. "See!" and then explained, "I wanted to talk about how things are going - to fill in Her Ladyship. She'll be on my case by tomorrow if I don't send her an update."

TD started. "I'd say mission accomplished. The guys have turned into professional drywallers in terms of the quality of the work. They don't work as fast as the pros, but they are rightfully proud of their work. They are united in spirit, and I think that was the point." He tipped his head back and for as though there was another side to the coin.

Now the pros working here likely wouldn't be that charitable. It really ticks off some of them who are all business, no chatter. I wonder if they know the name of the guy who is threading wire with them. You'd laugh at how the most minor thing will set off our guys on a tale from anywhere else, and of course, they have to stop to talk about it. Walking and chewing gum at the same time is not what they do. Doesn't matter. There is a pride that wasn't there before.

Winston agreed. "Our work on the professional suites on the first four floors will be all done when the painters finish. They're about halfway through that section. Then we can hand it over to the floor covering and furniture types. Meanwhile, the walling teams are up on the Lounge and Cafeteria level. That's been even more of a challenge getting the guys to work. Everyone wants to look out the windows. They spend their whole break time reminiscing, walking around and pointing out where they used to live. You'd hardly recognize them from the bunch of vagrants they were, living like trolls under the bridge a year ago. Nobody ever spent any time in a penthouse looking down on things below. They felt they were the things being looked down upon."

Jacob brought up the conversation he'd had with Bruce about the guys building an old guys' retirement home and Bruce's response. He'd just finished his summary when Bruce came out of the elevator and walked over to join them. He'd dropped into a chair as Winston and TD both laughed. "Tell Her Ladyship to find something else to worry about. Bruce was right. What's next?" They all exchanged greetings with Bruce.

"Talking about windows, what came out of that debriefing after the accident - where the guy fell over the edge? None of our guys were involved, were they?" He looked at TD

"If you ask me, it was Zid and Co making a point about keeping wayward in their extortion line. I heard that the guy who was pushed over had been delinquent in his payment. Of course, nobody asked me. But the story was that he had left too much slack in his tether. That's why he fell so far and wrecked his shoulder when he slammed back against the wall."

"The lift driver moving the window wall into place said he had the all-clear to move forward. He really can't see through the window wall with the dust and sunlight sometimes. Maybe the guy went where he shouldn't have to pick up a tool that was dropped. The window would have pushed it over the edge as it moved into place and could have dinged someone below. That's what some of his buddies said, but I think they were just covering for the driver. Anyway, everybody is back on schedule with even more safety protocols. But the anxiety factor has dropped a lot since Zid went homesick."

"That's news to me," said Jacob.

Winston picked up the story about how Zid had gotten a belly ache after lunch and then went home. TD nodded. "I heard him groaning in the toilet next to mine. I was having a pee before joining Pete to pick up pallets, sure sounded like that guy had fluid drive. I haven't seen him around since. Must be really sick."

"So the homes could start moving into place as soon as the cafeteria is up and running?" Jacob speculated.

"That's the plan - maybe three weeks TD said. The hallway lighting is going in. All the services are connected for levels five through nine and are ready for the containers to move up and into place. Its flex connections to the AC/heating system and return air, and then connecting the stack to the electrical wiring. Plumbing is an epoxy-fit hard connection to the sewer; flex connections for the hot and cold water. Might take half an hour if we're slow - a floor a day at least. The cable guys can hook up for TV and internet behind us."

Jacob sat stunned as he saw a dream realized. The guys had done it.

"What do the guys think, now that it's that close to finishing?" He looked at Bruce.

"I told you this before. Most of the guys have not looked past the next few days for a long time. They are having adjustment issues but are smiling as they do it. Having a house, however small, was not to be imagined a year ago. Hel-- Sorry." He almost caught his expletive in time. "A year ago, many were living under the bridge or squatting in an abandoned warehouse."

TD continued, "After we lift the houses into place, we're going to need some time to refocus. The job the guys were to do is over. We need to celebrate a bit and then set out the new expectations; we're not going to build homes to fill the rest of the building. Am I right? Each newbie will do their own with help from us." Jacob gave a slight nod.

"So we need to focus on the long-term plan. Some want to upgrade education or skills, and some want a job right now. They got an address to put on an application. Time to put the rest of the process into motion. Then, there is the plan to create an entertainment complex. Who is going to work on that? We can't use everyone."

Jacob pursed his lips. It was easy to see why TD had made a career in the military. Objective accomplished, move on to the next. Bruce seemed to sense what was bugging him.

"Well, the short-term objective was to build a unit through achieving a common objective," Bruce added. He, too, knew the jargon from similar training. But his work as a paramedic, when the term was used to indicate that he was the medical aid that dropped into battlefield situations on a parachute, made him aware of other dimensions. He paused to frame his words.

"I guess we have to ask if the unit we've become is strong enough to allow anyone else in. If we focus too tightly, we can only seem to be strong, you know. I can only admire the way the guys work together. They're like a blo-- Machine and proud to be so. The cracks are being filled before the last sheet is up, and before the mud is dry, the guys want to start sanding. Objective accomplished as long as we only wanted to become the Superior Drywall Company. What's buggin' Jake is that it looks like the church that kicked him out - rigidly focussed on a narrow world view. He was looking past this to the community we need to be in order to rescue any other street people like we used to be. Have I got that right, Jake?"

As Bruce articulated it, the pieces that had been jiggling about for so long in Jacob's mind snapped together. "Right enough. What I was hoping was that through this project, we could create something we all wanted but not so well that we forgot where we'd all been and how we might help others to join us. How do we keep doors open to bring others as needy as ourselves into the same security?"

TD seemed a bit confused. "Always was a limited objective type. Maybe it's my dark side." He seemed to shudder as unbidden thoughts tried to rise from where they were locked. "Could you expand on that a bit but not so much that I get lost?"

It was a gentle reminder, and Jacob did not miss the emphasis on the last word. "From my earlier life, I know there are a lot of people who have fallen through the cracks. My congregation was exemplary in looking after them. They could find scripture to justify their practice, just don't question who wrote it or when, or any other questions that come up if you study things too carefully. In the end, I carry that caring as their legacy. We know there are a lot of needy men not in our group; I see our next mission as finding and making a place for them within our community if they'd like to join it."

TD was thinking back to his military days and how a new recruit was brought into his group. "Well, there are a bunch of expectations you meet and a command structure, but there is nothing like manoeuvres to build the team."

"We've certainly done the manoeuvre thing," Jacob replied, but he wanted to get TD onto another track. "And it worked. So do we have a core on which to build? When new homeless come in, can we welcome them into our midst or do they just form another little clique?"

"If they follow the rules, what's the problem?" TD asked.

"It makes us exclusive, intolerant," Jacob blurted out without thinking. He caught himself and drew a breath, then continued more normally, "We may not have rules for new arrivals, or the rules might need to be changed," Jacob continued. "I once heard someone say that 'rules were for fools to obey and the guidance of wise men.'

"That was group captain Harry Day that said that," TD shot back immediately. "He had more medals than chest to pin them on. If anyone deserved the right to say it, he did."

"I thought it was Douglas Bader who said that," Bruce said.

"Group captain, Sir Douglas Bader, if you please, and he attributed the lines to Harry Day in his biography, you'll find," TD corrected, glaring at Bruce. Bruce looked across at Jacob as he received his criticism. "And that is a paraphrasing of the quote, but it has the idea," TD continued as he turned to look at Jacob.

"I am pleased to be informed," Jacob acknowledged, "but I was trying to make the point that there are others who are homeless, and this place could be a solution if we are flexible enough to let them in. As I recall, both Bader and Day carried war scars. I'm sure you know of current veterans who…" and stopped before he made too much of a point. He suddenly realized those across from him carried psychological scars of their military service. He'd been thinking of Pete as he started his rebuttal and only belatedly recalled the deep mental wounds his table mates carried.

"Anyways," he hurried on, "I was thinking of men with mobility issues and drug issues, besides the mental health problems, maybe on top of them. I think you get the idea. I wonder if the guys see themselves as part of the rehab of such others?"

"You could ask," Bruce offered. "Maybe when we start to eat together in the penthouse?" He laughed at the thought.

"*Me, eating in the penthouse! Never saw that coming!*" he thought.

They concluded their discussion with the decision to take a week off to let everybody get used to their new residences, and during that time, to talk about the next job(s). TD was first to leave.

Jacob was still shaking his head in confusion about how to get so many horses pulling in one direction when Bruce interrupted. "Did you think TD seemed a little abrupt? Like something was eating at him?"

"I think what worries him is not having a mission to accomplish. I've never seen him happier than when he's in the middle of something and when he's urging everyone on."

"Hmmm."

The communal job of first getting a home for each person built and then into place in the tower that had been a cover concealing private problems. With the mission completion, people relaxed and up bubbled those things that had been hidden. It kept Bruce, as the medical scout, busier than ever.

Harold wasn't the only hoarder. It was trying to relieve the panic of destitution that was really beyond his ability. But Bruce spotted them and got them into the right clinic, saw that they took their meds, kept a log on everyone on his list.

Harold and a friend got headed into building an archive. They had to learn computer skills so that they could be convinced into storing the actual newspapers, and etc. Jacob wondered if some of his students could help teach them without addicting them to games. He'd have to ask Maggie if that was an option. In the meantime, those guys were creating a library and resource centre from a set of four shipping containers that would go against the outside wall on the entertainment level.

Many of the men were working on building the raked seating for the auditorium that had grown to three floors, and that could double as a theatre. It would take up half of those top floors; the other half would become the workshop for building sets until someone figured out another use for the space. As it was, the idea of building sets for stages, even movie productions across the continent, was being studied, and the business plan developed by the high-priced help working in Lindsay Tower across the parking lot. The workers would build the sets and then pack them into shipping containers that would lower onto trucks below and motor off to wherever. It could appeal to the variety of skills the men had or had learned, and it offered options to inspire. Nobody had ever given any of the men, he knew, the chance to write a play or pursue any of the other writing arts.

*

But it was a rude awakening for Jacob to confront the fact that his looking outward was more than balanced by the cases of social collapse that sprang up. He had not appreciated the anxiety that constant companionship represented to some. Yes, they could hold up their end of a piece of drywall, but given the chance, they'd sooner find a quiet chair at home. Bruce had come up with the idea of convincing some of the guys to garden.

"This building is made of concrete, you know," TD felt he had to point out when Bruce made the suggestion, and Winston backed him up.

"Each guy gets a planter six feet on a side with a central support going up about five feet so they can grow a vertical garden as well. It will help to soften the hard spaces. This idea could take off, you know. Well, there are already requests for pets. One of the guys wants to raise pigeons if he can't have a parrot. He'd suggested it could fly free on his floor."

"How about a myna bird?" Winston suggested. "You can train them to talk, you know."

"We don't have enough talkers?" TD jested.

Bruce ignored the interruptions. "The problem is time. When I lived on the streets, all my time was taken up with survival - keeping safe or spotting the harm that was coming my way. I was always looking for a place to sleep, spotting something I might need, finding ways around the obstacles that bureaucracy put in my way. Sometimes I was looking out for a buddy who was sick or feeling bad. The point is, there was no time I remember that I could do something constructive. It wasn't living so much as trying not to die. Now all of that is gone. I haven't had it this good since the army. I get three meals a day. I got a job that pays and fills eight of twenty-four. Imagining what else I could do besides watch TV is a challenge. But because others are similarly afflicted, my spare time seems to have vanished."

"How's the schooling or training plan being received?" Jacob asked.

Winston replied, "Confidence is a big issue. Many are worried they might have burned out too many circuits, or the material they have to learn will be too hard. They've learned to be discouraged, and it's hard to unlearn. I think it will work better as they have a chance to talk about it, but they need someone successful in the circle as a model to keep the conversation from becoming a pity party. I think that is best accomplished at mealtime, and it is why a changing seating plan works better than seats that each feels he owns."

"In medieval times, this would be called a monastery," Jacob added. "But to get in, you had to be invited, and entry laid some heavy regs on you. Prayers five times a day, assigned tasks issued, a spartan existence for most. For that, you got a survival diet and the hope of everlasting life after you die."

I can see why the women banned religion in their community over there." TD nodded through the window at the tower across the parking lot.

"I'd better ask about female companionship. How's that working out?"

"Well, it is discreet," Bruce began. "So far, no complaints about being photo'd as an entry requirement. Some of the guys are beginning to talk about being allowed to have their children visit - though that's usually a spousal issue for a few for us. We have to expect a variety of mature relationships as time goes on and if it isn't a monastery."

"Don't get me talking about monasteries and that topic," Jacob huffed, and then in order to get off the matter, he added, "OK. Let's see about making some planter boxes available for anyone who wants or needs one. It should be easy enough to set them up under the LED lighting and even adjust the colours to make the stuff grow. Considering that the whole place never freezes, we could have the equivalent of a greenhouse here."

17

Thumb decided over one meal that he'd like to pick up the guitar again. He'd played it as a teenager, he claimed, and went on to describe the amped-up machine to which he'd retreat in the garage when the arguments started in the house. "Strumming it gave me this long digit," he claimed, then he hoisted the thumb that seemed to be twice as long as anyone else's and hooked like a broken spring. It set off a discussion about what music they all liked and whether they could find an instrument for TD. It showed up within the week. Bruce had been at the table when it happened and was telling Jacob and the others.

"You'd have been proud, Jacob. There was a moment when I thought mockery would take over. Maybe your posters in the elevator and up there are working." he nodded over the cafeteria about 'Giving and Receiving with Grace,' "They certainly have spawned enough jokes, but when Gary brought out the ukulele and presented it to Thumb, it was the moment of truth. I'm sure I caught Thumb's glance at the banner as he reached out to accept what Gary thought was a small guitar, like for a kid. Gary was so proud. He'd won the scavenger hunt. He had no idea it was a ukulele and not a guitar."

"And Thumb was touched. I mean, he had to look down for a moment to gather himself." Bruce had to pause to steady his own voice.

"Gary bragged how he'd found it in a pile of furniture being tossed out at an apartment building. The guys still can't pass a pile of stuff without looking it over."

"Hardly a scratch on it," Gary pointed out with a finger flip.

"Maybe I'm just getting sentimental, but you'd swear Thumb was taking a newborn when he reached across to accept it. Two hands out, big smile, the way he looked it up and down, almost counting fingers and toes. The table was as quiet as a church. I think some of the others were wondering what he would do."

"You're right," Thumb said. "This is what some guitarists start on to see if they really want to do strings. The strings are nylon, see, and when you press them, they don't hurt your fingertips. Guitar strings give you calluses. They're steel, and man, do you know if you haven't been practicing." He strummed it, and everyone laughed at how bad it was. But Thumb tuned it, and it sounded sweet. Mind you; the thing almost disappeared in his hands."

"It'll get me started, Gary, but I can tell you, sure as we're sitting here, by this day next month, I'm going to have me a full-sized guitar, Man. You've pushed me over the edge. I'm on my way." And he started wailing some song he said was from a Broadway show. I don't know it myself. Just the two lines - I'm on my way… to the Promised Land."

Winston couldn't help himself. "Gershwin … Porgy and Bess," he muttered.

It went around the table, each guy plinking it a bit. Thumb was showing how to hold it, how to strum with their thumb, how the sound changed when they pressed a string onto a fret. Jacob pulled out his daytimer and wrote in the date three weeks away to ask Thumb about his guitar and a separate name of someone who he knew was a program coordinator at the community centre near the Mall.

"How's the gardening project going?" Jacob asked. "From what I see, it started well. I mean, the residential spaces almost look like streets."

Winston wanted to follow up. "First, lettuce has been added to salads. I just wish more would eat the stuff. I think these guys are gaining weight and are passing optimum size. There's no problem getting rid of desserts, but we need a program on eating veggies if we're to head off the bad things that come with diabetes and all."

"Can we use some of the expertise that the women have in the hydroponic garden they have under the parking lot?" Jacob asked.

"I've been wondering if we could build a bunch of hydroponic boxes for lack of a better word. Maybe set them up in the lounge and cafeteria area. We have these big hard spaces," he waved his hand around the lounge area that had comfortable seating but nothing else, "that need something besides a poster and potted palms. We could grow tomatoes and beans, maybe radishes, onions, some herbs right at the table area." He waved a hand to an empty space. "Hey, pick me that tomato, eh?".

"Would it set off a war?" TD interjected. "Hey, that's my tomato; I've been looking after it since it was a baby. Food fights?" It was a typical contribution to be somehow linked to war, but it came as a surprise. Lately, TD had attended the gatherings but not said much. Bruce was convinced something was wrong, but he'd been told he was imagining things at each inquiry.

"Maybe we have to talk about that," Winston suggested. "Maybe it becomes a related kitchen duty to pick the veggies. But someone else would have to plan, plant, and grow them. We'd need to work out a study to see what we could count on. The kitchen staff can advise and give an idea of amounts they'd need, but they are already busy enough with meal prep and cleanup."

"I think we'd better bring the heating and cooling engineers into this loop if we go ahead," Jacob offered. "There surely would be humidity and heating issues they'd need to compensate for. Maybe they'd suggest where to set up a test plot best if it is going to supply the kitchen."

"I'll look into it," Winston offered, and the others nodded.

18

The ukulele band took off like a rocket, and of course, Gary became the pilot. Jacob had heard that the community centre had just started such a group. When he convinced a bunch of the guys to come over with him one night to 'try it out', they each returned with a beginner's instrument they could now afford and an obligation to meet for half an hour before or after supper depending on who was working where and the evening TV schedule. The business books called it 'team building'.

Tom was a part of the group for now, but finding an acoustic guitar was dividing his loyalties. Gary was part of the team creating the auditorium in the tower, so he had time that some others in the band used for travel to off-site jobs to practice. And he did. It was only a surprise to him that he found he didn't need to watch his fingers after a while to put them on the right strings and frets. Everyone else who watched the passion he put into the hobby was surprised that he was surprised.

"Did you not expect to get better?" Jacob heard one of the band ask one night. "I mean, if you've done the thing a hundred times, would you not expect your fingers to find their own way?" The newfound confidence led Gary far past the rest in a matter of weeks, but rather than to learn a whole lot of new pieces; he chose to explore every way possible to play what the others were. "Let's play that repeat slowly, or more softly… no really softly," he urged them. He also took to writing up new words to the melodies the band learned.

Jacob winced when he heard what Gary had in mind. All he could imagine would be coming were crude lyrics to a ballad. When the expected didn't happen, he realized he'd been trapped by his own… well, bigotry. "Let's call a spade a shovel," he admitted to himself. He still had not crossed from thinking that street people were foul-mouthed by definition.

What Gary turned out were lovely lyrics, and it became apparent why he'd wanted to have the band play softly, and slowly, or loudly through the same passages. He matched the words that must already have been in his mind to those musical expressions.

Jacob was sitting near Thumb on the first night Gary handed out new words to one song they had learned well. The plan was to take it to the community centre group practice and offer to do it as a solo within the group thing. He thought he heard T groan audibly as soon as the paper came out. Thumb asked for a bathroom break. He stayed away long enough for the band practice to end. Hockey called to some. Thumb returned to collect his instrument.

"Not feeling well?" Jacob asked.

"I'm OK," Thumb said with the conviction of a three-dollar bill.

"You might do a solo spot in that song on your guitar," Jacob suggested. "I'll bet Gary would even write special words for you. This is really nice stuff he's written, isn't it?"

Thumb turned abruptly after snapping his case closed. "Jake, I don't know how to learn those words."

Jacob jerked back in surprise.

Thumb shook his head in frustration. "Jake, I can't read!" he said so quietly Jacob almost missed the admission.

He snatched up his own case and quick-stepped to join Thumb, who was obviously opting for the stairs down through the empty levels to his own place. Obviously, he was avoiding the others in the band who had lined up awaiting the elevator.

"Whoa, whoa," Jacob called as he caught up two floors down. It was as empty and as private as you'd find in the building. Thumb was leaning on the rail, looking out the window at the lights below. He didn't wait for Jacob to ask silly questions.

"I've never been able to read," Thumb began. "When they started writing stuff on the board, it was all scribbles to me. When they asked us to read something, I'd read back what I'd memorized. Teachers do that all the time. They tell you what they're going to do; then they do it, and then they tell you what they told you. It must be in some teaching book. Anyway, if you pay attention the first time, you got the rest of the time to figure out how to duck their questions and if you can't, you hold up the notebook you're supposed to have written in, and just say what the teacher told you to put in it. I just filled my book with doodles.

"So, how did you learn to play the guitar?" Jacob asked.

"Well, you don't have to read a word. Just try it out, see what works."

"But you know the words to all those songs you sing."

"Good memory from listening to them enough."

They stood beside each other, looking out at the dark space below.

"If I read the words, could you memorize them?"

"You might have to do it a lot."

"Well, I'd have to know them myself. I'd just be doing them with a friend. Call it motivation for me... sort of like the way you helped Gary get started with the ukulele."

"It might be easier for me to just drop out of the band - do my guitar thing."

"Maybe, but then you'd have to explain why I don't know the words. I'd lay the blame squarely on you, you know."

Thumb looked at him askance.

"So, did you offer me a beer at your place so we could start on words?"

"Sure," said Thumb with resignation. But Jacob could hear the fear beneath.

Thumb had replaced the mailbox each person had been offered with an old-fashioned chalkboard. Jacob could tell it was real slate, enclosed in a painted, wooden frame. A clear plastic cup of chalk pieces was hanging on a screw in the frame. A finger down behind the top of the frame snagged a long twist tie. With that twist tie, he jerked his house key from a hidden slot in the back of the top. He opened his door and replaced the key, then invited Jacob in.

As soon as he closed the door, he strode to the front window and pulled the curtains. Not even light from the corridor street outside penetrated.

"Just a minute," Thumb said into the darkness and flipped on a light. He pulled out an abused, pressed-back, antique chair with arms from the table for Jacob to sit. The large TV screen each place came with commanded attention, Thumb's unit hung on a ceiling pivot. It commanded the space. Jacob was settling into his chair as he admired the novel setup.

That's a great idea," Jacob complimented. "It acts like a room divider over top of your dresser unit. "Each residence came with eight modular cupboard units that were about four feet wide, two feet deep and four feet high for storage of everything. Stack 'em, or put them back to back, side by side or end up. That's all you got. And one got used for a sink if you wanted it.

"Come on back," Thumb invited.

Jacob went to where Thumb was reaching into a bar fridge, below the counter, for two cans of ale. He glanced up then sideways to measure the space. "I see you put the bed on pulleys." It was no problem for Thumb, but Jacob felt like the ceiling was awfully close.

"Yeah, I don't need the bed taking up floor space when I want to be in here. And when I sleep, I don't need the kitchen." The kitchen had a microwave and toaster oven side by side at shoulder height over the sink. They had been huge haggle items at the time when the residences were being planned.

"What do they need them for if they eat in the cafeteria?" complained the financial people who were tasked with creating and adhering to the project budget.

"Well, anyone wants to have a friend over sometime. With these, they can have a pizza or TV dinner in private. Sort of like you guys can go home for a private meal," TD had said acidly. The meeting had moved on immediately, Jacob recalled.

Thumb set the cans beside the sink and reached the over-counter unit to his right for two glasses. "If I never have beer from a can again, it will be too soon. I doubt you'll remember, but when we had that Christmas dinner over in the other tower, and I asked you if I could take my beer glass home, you said I could. I noticed when you put your IOU in the dishwashing tray to explain its absence. Never forgot that. That was a generous thing to do for some bum off the street. Anyways, when I moved in here, I vowed I'd never serve beer in a can again, and I think of you every time I pour a glass.

Jacob was a bit flustered. "I'm glad to be part of a fond memory. Not everyone remembers me that way." He was thinking back to the congregation that had fired him for his liberal theology.

Thumb was pouring the beer down the side of the glasses; both found themselves listening to the slight hiss. "How did you come up with that end cupboard?" Jacob was pointing to an eight-foot columnar cupboard at the end of the counter and beside the door to the bathroom. "That wasn't part of the standard package."

"Well, if you cut off these two," he pointed to the one with the sink and the other that made the other side of the L along the bathroom wall, "they are about thirty inches high, and the overhead one, so it gives you headspace over the counter, you have enough to make that."

Jacob raised his glass in salute. "Well done. Cheers."

"Iechjyd Da," Thumb said in return. It raised Jacob's eyebrows.

"It's Welsh," Thumb explained. "That's my heritage" It means 'Good Health.'"

"Say it again. Never heard that one."

Thumb repeated the greeting that began with a sound like he was clearing his throat.

Jacob tried it until he got it. "Can't say my community had greetings to share over a mug of ale. It was forbidden fruit, so I go around collecting greetings from the guys whenever they invite me. Do you mind if I write that down?" He headed back to the chair and table under the front window, pulling out his daytimer as he went.

Thumb followed after he had rotated the TV screen, so it looked into the living area. He flipped it on and quickly moved through channel options to the one from the rotating camera feed on the roof.

"I love looking at that view," Thumb said.

As Jacob looked up from his book, he felt a moment of vertigo as though the place might be moving. It passed as soon as he blinked and took a deep breath. He sat and picked up his glass.

Thumb pulled another almost matching chair from its place at the other end of the table. His had a piece of stout doweling replacing a carved leg.

Jacob dug out his copy of the new words that Gary had created and spread them on the table. Thumb groaned gently.

"I'm sorry you have had such an awful time with reading. If you want, there are tricks you can learn that will help, and there are audiobooks all over the place if you are interested."

Thumb waved his words away and took another big sip. "Why don't you read me a line?"

Jacob did. Thumb repeated it. They backed and forth a couple of times, then moved to the following line. When they went back to do both lines together, each made different mistakes.

"Let's try this." Thumb drained his glass and reached behind him for his guitar case. He checked and tuned the instrument and then played the first line of the melody from memory.

"It'll be better for me to play. I can connect the words, then to the music. I don't know how that works, but it does for me."

In minutes both could sing the first verse correctly.

"Enough, for tonight," Thumb announced. "Come by tomorrow night, maybe?"

"Good idea," Jacob agreed.

Thumb broke into his rendition of 'Streets of Laredo". ... as I walked out on Laredo one day," he crooned sweetly. "I spied a young cowboy all wrapped in white linen…"

Jacob listened to the end and stood. "See you tomorrow."

Thumb stood and held out his hand. When Jacob gripped it, Thumb said, "Everybody calls me Tom Thumb. You can call me Owen... Owen Jones."

Jacob nodded with a smile. He knew when a curtain had been lowered. "Iechjyd Da," he said and got the correct, back-of-the-throat sound.

Owen nodded and smiled.

Jacob was halfway through the door when he stopped and turned back. "Owen, if you can't read, why do you have a chalkboard at the door?"

"For notes from somebody who came by, of course."

"But you can't read them," Jacob said.

"We're talking about different notes, I think. If you want to say you were by and leave me a note, do it this way."

He picked a stub of chalk from the holder and slashed a stack of five horizontal lines - a musical staff. A swirl indicated it was a treble clef. "You do know the musical lines and spaces, don't you? For 'Jacob' we could use 'quarter rest',' a', 'c', rest, 'b'. If you're feeling down, put it in the bass clef." He scribbled what he meant. "If you're feeling up, go up an octave." Again he repeated the pattern. "If it's an emergency, use eighth notes or sixteenth's with two tails. I'll call you back. What more would you expect to say in a note pinned on a door?"

Jacob laughed at himself. *I've written too many sermons,* he thought.

19

When Jacob returned the next night, Thumb's planter had arrived. The guys in the shop that were planning to build stage scenery had begun with something simple and repetitive. Six-foot square bins three feet high made of beige, pressure-treated lumber seemed to fill the bill.

There was a double bottom in the planter. The upper one was perforated and was only to keep two feet of soil in place and up off the floor. The layer below was solid, watertight, and sloped to direct any excess watering out the side through a spigot. "That hole has to be near the floor drain, you guys," the placement team was advised by Winston. "Don't cover the drain. There are lots of reasons why water might appear on the floor besides careless watering. We need to be able to find the drains." The men had done their job well based on the unit in front of Thumb's place.

It was decided everyone could have one, but some chose to donate theirs to the lounge/cafeteria area. What you could grow in it was dictated by those who would prepare the food. They could allow flowers, but there were some things whose growth was not to be permitted. You could ask for a pyramidal support if you wanted it. It was pointed out that it could support beans, roses, and cucumbers, or you could go for an ornamental tree or nothing at all. Thumb had asked if he could plant Haskap bushes to provide a fruit that looked and tasted like a blueberry-raspberry cross. "They're well known out west, where I come from," he had said. "You need two kinds for cross-pollination," he had added.

"What does cross-pollination mean?" asked one of his neighbours. When Thumb explained, Rajik said, "I should have known that; I think I did once. It must be these meds I'm on. I don't feel so down, but it's like I feel mixed up and don't care."

It's why we have these small bumblebees," Thumb continued. They buzz about, moving pollen around from flower to flower. One of the guys suggested them instead of bees. We don't need as many of them as bees, and they don't bother with people. Bees, the ones that make honey, take a lot of effort and attention. These guys don't."

Rajik was the one who asked which way was up when he planted his bean seeds.

"Someone's been pulling your leg on that one too, Rajik," Thumb said. "Seeds are a bit like you. They are always to land on their feet. No matter how you plant them, they all seem to get their roots growing down and stems grow up. You know you're going to be really impressed when you see what a little care will do for these. I'm looking forward to coming over for the first picking."

Thumb knew that Rajik was having a tough time with depression. Bruce had suggested he use a planter to give him something to look forward to. He'd asked Thumb to help with the planting.

With Thumb's help, Rajik had planted yellow and green bush beans and saved his vertical support for training cucumbers. He showed him how to draw a finger through the soil and line up the seeds about a hand's breadth apart, then cover and pat the soil as you would pat a child you'd put to bed. By the time they'd worked their way around the planter and then poked holes for the cucumber seeds in the hills in the middle, Rajik was moving comfortably and confidently.

"You just watch those things grow," Thumb had said. He pointed to the communal watering can hanging above the spigot installed beside the fire hydrant. "Get water from the tap over there, and I'll show you how to soak these seeds down to get them started. It'll take a few cans this time because we have to soak the soil below. After that, it might only be a can full a couple of times a week till we see a lot of leaves."

Rajik headed off, as directed. When he lugged back a full can, Thumb showed him how to gently soak the soil, move on to another spot, then come back for a re-soaking. "It keeps you from washing out the seeds." When they stepped back, there was a flat expanse of wet dirt.

"Doesn't look like much but give it a week," Thumb said. "Oh. Put the can back on the hook. The other guys will need it." As they walked to do that, Thumb said, "If this were a workday, it would be break time. Want to go for a coffee upstairs?"

With his task complete, Rajik looked like a deflating balloon. "I think I'll sit alone for a while." He shoved his hands in his pockets, probably to wipe the wetness off, and must have found a toked that reminded him to say something there. "Thanks for helping me, Thumb," he said.

Thumb escorted him back across the hallway to his place. A folded chair stood beside the door. "Maybe you could sit out and watch the world go by, Rajik." He pulled open the chair and steadied it while Rajik sat down.

"I'll be off now," Thumb said, waving. As he climbed the stairs to the level above, Gary was coming down. They greeted each other in passing. Thumb called after him, "Talk to Rajik while he's out. Ask him about planting the seeds."

"Got him."

20

Jacob was reporting to Maggie as his Fridays required. He'd not met her on the elevator, and because of that, the update that might have been a few minutes was now looking like an inquisition.

"I'm pleased to hear how well the group is getting along. So, when are the others who don't belong to the boy's club going to be welcomed in? Homeless men are still being pictured on the streets, and there are," she glanced at the ceiling as she sorted a mental file, "Ahhh... eight empty floors are there not? That's room for about a hundred more." She paused with eyebrows lifted, waiting for a reply.

"I saw that picture of the new encampment under the bridge in the paper too. Must satisfy some fundamental needs to find the people with the same difficulties are drawn to similar spots time and again. It attracted some attention from the guys who wondered who it was that had their old corner. For most, it was a quick turn to the next page. Been there, done that. No need for a t-shirt. Anyways, to answer your question, I first need to talk to the guys and then depending on that, make overtures to those in that photo."

"Jacob," Maggie said with enough steel in her voice to make her point, "this is not their option. They can't monopolize a building that is two-thirds empty. That might have been the case when they slipped into the back door of a warehouse; it isn't here. Those other men have as great a need for housing as they do. So move them along."

Jacob thought of Bruce's retort and just nodded instead.

*

It was some of the guys who christened the dinner a Thanksgiving one, and Jacob drew a sigh of relief because it gave him at least a familiar platform upon which to make his appeal. In his old congregation, he'd have collected all the scriptural references together in praise for the bountiful harvest that someone else had had so that they could be fed through the coming winter. In this group, he would lean on the fellowship that had grown up among them. When he stood and called their attention, they all seemed to know something was up.

"I'm pleased that we all could be here for this dinner. I've been listening to you trade your stories of where you were this time last year. We have much to be thankful for." He scanned the room and named those on afternoon or night shifts who were missing; He nodded his thanks to

Thumb, who had convinced Rajik to bring up part of his bean harvest to the dinner and stay to eat it among the others. It still made Rajik anxious to be amongst so many, but he was making headway, and Jacob hoped that the gardening and community support encouraged the man's recovery.

"I need to bring up the next step in our evolution as a group," Jacob continued. "You've all seen the article about the newly displaced men living under the bridge and in like places around town. As winter comes in, you all know how the cold will grip their arthritis," a few squirmed at the thought, "and how the thought of a warm and safe place would appeal to them. I want that place to be here, and I need your help in welcoming them." A few nodded their heads; more turned to mutter, "so that's what this is about? No free lunch, is there?"

Jacob barged on. "Somehow, I need you guys with whom I've shared so much to become more than you are, maybe more than you want to be, by bringing these others out there, in here." He waved his hand in the direction of the bridge outside and twenty floors down, then tapped the table.

"Now, we've made up rules that seem to have served us well. I don't see them changing, but I need you to help me plan how to integrate those others into our group. Nobody knows better how to do this. I doubt there is a problem out there that somebody here hasn't overcome and could share a pathway forward. But we need to help those guys find what you did. I think it would be helpful if we offered each person who wants to come in from the cold the chance to build his own place as you did, with the help of all of us, as we did for each other." There was general nodding and sounds of agreement.

"We'd need some sort of selection process," a voice said from the floor. "I'm not about to invite some junkie or dealer in." Everyone knew of the speaker's ongoing efforts to stay clean. "I don't need no temptation," he declared, and there was loud agreement around him in support. It set loose a chorus of undesirable behaviours they didn't want to see. TD held up his hand in the noise, and Jacob called on him. The chatter dropped immediately.

"Maybe a couple of us could visit them and tell them about this place - sort of like ambassadors. We've finished the auditorium, so we have the manpower to do that and then help with shipping container construction for those who pass."

That seemed to be agreeable to the group and encouraged Jacob to get to the crux of the issue. "Whoever joins our group, the question will be where they get to stay. Do we isolate them on new floors, or do we integrate them into our midst, a few on each floor? It would mean our team would be spread over different floors, but I think that would be the best idea. We don't need to create two competing factions. We need to remain one community, and it will be the best we can do to keep everyone successful. Because we are so unique, any backsliding will be noticed and used to denigrate us all. We become yet another failed effort to outsiders. We don't need that. But to advance and open up all the space, we need to figure out how this group will open to admit others. It is a matter for another time... but not too long." He hoisted the dregs in his glass, and others did immediately. The chorus of good wishes was as good as it would get.

21

TD, Bruce and Jacob went down to the bridge on the weekend. They took their welcome with them in the form of hot coffee takeouts. Jacob thought that they might have been expected judging from the fact that there seemed to be so many, and the attitude seemed curious, only a little hostile.

"Are you reporters?" asked one. "We didn't like getting our pictures in the paper."

"No fear," TD said. "I just came to see who had my spot. He pointed to a spot high on the slope near the abutment. "I slept for months up there. My name's TD. He's Bruce, and this guy is Jake. Bruce and I lived here a year back--" He was cut off by a surly voice.

"Well, you ain't getting it back! It's mine now." The vagrant was heavy and stood slowly. "That's my stuff there. You gotta find somewhere else."

"Man, you are welcome to it," TD said, hand out. "I just know how cold it can be when the weather changes, like now. Plus, I found a better place anyway. What we came to do was offer you a place to join us. We got room, and it's warm and safe."

"You said your name was TD?" another interrupted. "Do you know Pete? ...or a guy we call the Hat?"

"You mean the guy who used to collect beer cans in a shopping cart and the guy with the awful top hat? Yeah, I know them. They're part of the group that I live with."

"I heard of you, then." He turned to the others and said. "He's OK."

"I don't recall you from the shelter?" asked another.

"Got out of there a long time ago—too many bedbugs. Don't know what it's like now. That's why I had that spot up there. I could deal with cold, not crawly things." The comment brought chuckles, and the group edged a little closer, relaxed a bit.

"So Jake here is the guy who runs the place where we live now, and he's here to invite you to join us. He did the same for me and the others back about last Christmas, and it's worked out well. There is space for more in our situation, and you guys came to our attention because of the newspaper picture."

Jake stepped forward. "What we offer is a place that is safe and warm. We offer you a community that moves away from the circles or spirals that most of us are caught in. Each group member has built themselves a home out of shipping containers that are provided. We've each helped each other to make a clean place with your own bathroom, a kitchen if you want, and a TV. Your place and daily cafeteria meals are paid for by your welfare cheques or out of your wages if you work off-site. Everyone is expected to do work for the community. I said to the others that if they wanted to join that I wanted their soul in exchange. I shocked myself when I said that, but it has worked out that way. All those guys were like you. They were the dropouts or driven outs of every level of society. They can tell you all day of the frustrations that stood in their way of finding life beyond despair. But they all took a leap of faith. They joined to create this place and their place in it. They invite you to join them because they have made what they think you are seeking - but it isn't free. You have to commit to something beyond yourself.

"Jake used to be a preacher," TD interrupted, and the explanation drew a chuckle. "Here's what my container looked like when I started." He called up a picture on his phone and walked around. "Here's what it looks like now, outside. He walked back. "And finally inside," one more trip across the group.

"You built that... yourself?" gasped one man incredulously.

"Nope." I was on the team that did the strapping, interior drywall and paint for everyone's place. Some of the other guys did the electrical, plumbing and exterior. It was just an efficient way to do things. After you've learned how to do it, you got better and more confident as you did it more. So that is what you'd be doing. We'd team you up with guys who know how to do it, and in less than a month, you can have a place to call your own."

"Would it really be mine?" asked a new voice.

"Yes. You'll have to commit to a three-year term in the group, and you'll pay a reasonable rent for your slot that will include buying your place. At that point, you can leave with your home on a flatbed to put it in any place that will let you build a foundation. We'd hope you keep in touch, but we're all big guys now. Life can move on. This isn't expected to be a retirement home."

"So what's the downside?" asked the new voice again.

"Well, you have to commit to working for the group, and as Jake says, you must give and receive help with grace. That's not a person; it's an attitude. The foul language disappears, the smoking, drugs, booze and gambling disappears. You find new ways to get those highs you are looking for. The new highs don't leave you feeling gypped, and they don't come out of a bottle or syringe.

"Will you help me get clean?" a small voice asked.

"If you want, but we don't give you a tool until you are. And quite honestly, you will find daily work in a team exhausting once you are. But we have done it with others; we could do it with you. That's Bruce's angle here. He used to be a paramedic in the armed forces. He's our on-site medic, and he connects you to the high-priced help you need. He's a good guy, but if you want to come to start a pity party for yourself - don't bother."

"I guess that's the last thing," Bruce suggested. He was rudely interrupted.

"You got any ready-made apartments? I'm ain't living in no fuckin' shipping container."

TD looked at him square on. "Absolutely not. Sorry. If you aren't interested in building something with help, you can go back to that place you staked out up there." He nodded to the dip in the ground where a sleeping bag was rolled up on slabs of cardboard. "We'd be glad to talk with you about the weather any time we see you on the street. Don't tell me your problems, though. If you join the groI wishwe can see you through them. Wish we were perfect and could promise you the end of your troubles, but we can't. However, forty-eight of us have done it together already and so far. If you join us, we all have work to do. If you don't, no problem. Nice knowin' ya'." He turned back to Bruce. "You were about to say..?" The challenger had leaned back and lost his smile.

"I was going to say, you might want to talk about your own situation and whether you're ready to do this. Some of you may have been down so long you can't imagine anything else. You've been through every bureaucrat in town. You've been jerked around and feel exploited for so long it's what everywhere is. But if you have questions, we'll be in the tent in the twin towers' parking lot," - he hooked a thumb over his shoulder, "from six till eight each night this week. Bring anyone else that might be interested. Most of us weren't homeless but felt as though we were, based on the hovels we had to live in. Don't know if others filled those spaces and want to get out of them too. You got till next week to make up your mind. After that, we're working with those who took the chance. We won't be able to help you after that till next year."

The group broke up into pairs to talk about what they heard. Jacob noticed Bruce go over to the guy who asked if he'd get help to get clean.

"You said you wanted some help. Bruce is my name. What's yours?" Bruce asked.

"Eustache," the skinny man answered. He was already showing signs of nervous anxiety.

Jacob looked away. He felt like a voyeur. Across the group, TD took the big guy who had challenged him aside. He thought TD slipped him some money. "Kind gesture," Jacob thought.

During the week, TD, Bruce and Jacob got some of the others to come down to the tent. On a couple of nights, they even held ukulele practice there, and it was the music that pulled or pushed some into saying 'I do.' Bruce found a couple of men who had pneumonia. He phoned the pharmacy in the women's tower to say he was sending two over for antibiotics.

They were husky guys both coughing up phlegm and wheezing like steam engines. "Can you make it over there?" Bruce asked. "Yeah," one answered for both. "See you on Friday here after supper," Bruce said. They both stood and shuffled out. But three men showed up at the pharmacy.

"I was asked to make sure they made it," the young, unshaven man said. The pharmacist had the antibiotics ready in bottles for the older guys. "Bruce said he was busy but would call over my prescription for Percocet, but you could give it to me right now. It's for 100."

The pharmacist had Bruce on speed dial and was waiting for him to pick up when the young man started to reach into his pocket. He hadn't pulled whatever it was out before one of the old guys reached across the kid's front, grabbed his shoulder and spun him around to face a fist like a boxing glove. The old guy's spittle sprayed the other's face as he said in his Scottish brogue, "Thanks for your help, friend, now bugger off before you really need that pain killer. I think the man said he wanted to talk to you again before he wrote up an order for that stuff."

The other old guy had stepped up close behind the younger and already had a clamp on his arm that was holding whatever it was in his pocket. There was a momentary flare of anger in the younger man's face before it collapsed and he ran out of the store.

"Hi, Bruce?" said the pharmacist as he turned back to the counter. "I have a younger man here who says... where did he go?"

"He got mixed up," the older man said, unclenching his fist as he turned back from the figure running out the door. "The doctor told him to come back tomorrow. Thanks for this, though." He reached for one of the green plastic bottles in front of the pharmacist.

"Just a minute," the pharmacist said. "Bruce said when he called me that he wanted you to start that right now." He drew two small paper cups of water from the tap in the sink on his counter and tapped out two capsules for each man. "Take two now and every meal tomorrow."

When he realized they might not eat at regular hours, he continued. "Bedtime and each mealtime - that's morning, noon and night, and then at bedtime - every four hours. That's really important if you're going to catch that germ. It can kill you, you know."

"Thanks," they both said and slugged down their pills and left.

*

"Thirty-five signed up," Jacob reported to Maggie when she stopped by the tent late on Friday night. She'd sat apart doing emails on her phone as the final vagrants came in to commit. Her head went up when the two with pneumonia came in to report to Bruce. It was their coughs that caught her attention. Though she'd been a head nurse in her youth and had long since been doing philanthropy instead, she still had her ear for a severe cough. She asked him about them when she joined them and before Jacob could give his report.

"Those two..."

"Pneumonia," Bruce cut her off. "Fourth day on antibiotics, and they've turned the corner. They'll be OK by next week."

"Do they want in?"

"Yep," Bruce replied. "Names are Blake and Byron," he shuffled his papers, "...Smythe. Brothers, if not twins, Scottish by ancestry by their brogue. They asked if they could be together in one place. I said we could work out a side-by-side placement of their own homes. I think there are big dependency issues there, but we'll see.

"They'll need follow-up--"

"Got 'em, Maggie. Already on my list."

"Sorry, Jacob. You were saying. Thirty-five new candidates?"

"Yes, and they come with issues we've ignored until now. Dexter, Dex for short, has a motorized scooter. He walked into the tent, and we collected his info. Then he admitted that walking across the tent is as far as he can make it. So admitting him will require a review of all doorways, exit procedures, elevator clearances, and certainly a refit of his house." Everyone turned to Dan for a comment on the plans.

Dan stared at the ceiling of the tent for a moment. "OK, the bathroom wall will need to be moved forward unless grab bars would meet his need. If he can leave the scooter outside, that would be better. It might be that he has to take it inside where he is because he's afraid it would be stolen." Everyone nodded.

"If it has to come inside, he'll have to have a single bed,

not the queen size everyone else has. Maybe it should tip-up. He'd need a ramp to get in. It probably would have to have a bend in it to fit the space between residences. Likely a wider doorway. Still, it's doable," he concluded. Everyone was ready to move on when he raised his stump to add, "it's the emergency exit plan that will need to be checked. I suspect that the stairways through the office levels will need to be changed to ramps for his scooter to negotiate. That'll lose you some office space because the ramps have to be longer." Jacob noted Maggie's ceiling stare and frown.

"So the cost of having him here is rather high," Maggie said.

"Well, yes, but it was one of the things that got missed initially. Had I arrived with no leg, maybe it would have been fixed during construction. How hard is it to improve the business plan?

"Harder than you think," Maggie replied. "Let's deal with that later. You said there were some other problems."

Jacob nodded to Bruce. "Pets are the big one," Bruce said. "A couple have dogs they want to bring. The topic of overnight female visitors and children visitors on days when they have visiting rights are the new ones. There are some with dietary issues and some mental health issues, but nothing we haven't dealt with already."

"It's late now. We should deal with the last two at a group meeting. Have you figured out the changes of locations and which guys are willing to share a floor with the new arrivals?"

"In progress," said Jacob.

"I'll be off then," Maggie said. "Update next week?", she asked looking at Jacob. "I'll be able to talk to the financial types and engineer re the ramps by Monday. Go ahead and get the containers delivered before mid-week."

\*

Jacob had to acknowledge the reluctance of the groups to open to new members. As he walked home, he reflected on his original invitation for Winston to come to live at his house. That had been a spontaneous decision, and it had worked out well. Even when Winston moved out to join the others at the tower, Jacob had still kept his house, and the professional distancing it allowed, rather than join the rest of the men in the 'modern monastery,' as the guys called it. He'd heard it more than once. "It's exactly what they'd have done in medieval times if they had had structural steel. But the containers would be the size of closets in those days," they joked.

Well, the discussion had been stressful. Having just settled in and gotten some feeling of permanence, it was time to disrupt things again. No wonder it was so hard to get them to address the problem. And he wasn't going to move out of his house in the process. Fine example!

It was TD who came to his rescue, yet again. Jacob had noticed his fidgeting on the edge of his own anxiety. Where

Jacob found himself agonizing about what words to say to try and inspire a sense of magnanimous altruism that might have appealed to a convention of well-heeled academics, TD was scanning the crowd and ticking off talents. He was choosing his men for an operation just the way he had done in the military units he had been part of and commanded in the past. TD jumped to his feet after half an hour of dithering and excuses. "There's a bigger mission here, Men," he had shouted. "We're the beachhead." The room went silent when he said that.

"Remember where we were a couple of years ago? Bouncing around like flotsam, trying to keep our heads above water. Then out of the mist, we saw what looked like solid ground. We washed up here and worked like mad to secure the landing, and we did, but we all knew that we were the vanguard. The reinforcements are coming ashore, and we're not going to turn around and start shooting at them, are we? They're the good guys, and some are more beat up than we were. So let's figure out how we're going to make sure they don't die on the beach. I think we should break up into platoons and occupy the whole building. Each group has a communications specialist, an engineer or two to build bridges and lay out roadways. We need someone to be sure supplies and medical issues are covered and keep us strong. Lastly, each group needs a bunch of grunts to make it happen. This isn't rocket science. Create groups that cover those bases and get ready to deploy in two weeks." He sat down and waited.

The room was silent for a while after that. People were looking at each other, deciding who they most liked to be with, what they could do from the list of tasks tossed at them before someone gave them a job they didn't want. Then the chat started, and people were leaning over and across. A few beckoned others.

Jacob seized the moment. "Let's see what TD's idea looks like. Let's group ourselves into twelve groups, and we'll identify them by floor number. This table will be floor five," and his arm arced across the room, pointing at tables and numbering them up to floor sixteen. He caught himself before he tried to place people on the auditorium floors and penthouse cafeteria.

The men got up and muddled about. There were the inevitable several who were last to be chosen, and it was eventually decided that they'd form eleven groups. There was surprising superstition about being on floor thirteen. Jacob was surprised to find himself making Biblical connections to the Apostles. Maybe the thirteenth floor was the 'time out' floor where mismatched groups could find a solution.

Suddenly, people were making schedules to move their homes on the hoist; the ukulele group practices were reduced so that they could start to work on planting boxes that would now be needed for the other floors. And rationing was set up that matched number of units to the production that was possible in the time available. Suddenly it looked like the D-Day landing.

His mental review brought Jacob to his front door. He found himself recalling the maxim about idle hands being the devil's playhouse or something like that. He slid his key into the lock and opened it into a silent space. "It is so quiet after the meeting," he thought and just as he was sighing and thinking there was a nightcap calling his name from the kitchen, he recalled he didn't have his lesson prepared for school tomorrow.

## 22

The lesson started on the patio outside the cafeteria on the top floor of Lindsay Tower, where they could look down on the collection of newly delivered shipping containers. Jacob explained how they were being transformed into apartments. One of the second-year students explained that it was the modern-day equivalent of Diogenes living in a wine barrel. They all knew the story.

"It is making use of a resource that is currently not needed," Jacob explained. "We import many more finished goods than we produce here, and all that stuff comes from overseas in these containers. That stuff can't be sent in the quantities needed, just in cardboard boxes. Can you imagine why?"

The kids could and did.

"If we made more stuff that those countries wanted, we could send it back in these containers, but the fact is, we don't. So every year, there are a bunch of these containers that have to be recycled or cut up, melted down and turned into something else. We've bought them to make into apartments. Today we're going for a return visit to the site to follow things with the new group of men who are working on them. And I want to see if you can discover the other uses the containers are supposed to be fulfilling."

Dan, with the mangled hand from an industrial accident, was their guide. He explained how it had happened and the limitations it had imposed on his life thereafter. It was why he was their guide, but he was able to read the drafting drawings that others couldn't. So he was making sure all the walls, electrical, plumbing, and heating were in the correct place. He took them to one unit that was being fitted with the vertical studs to which exterior siding would be attached.

"Start with the idea that you have to insulate these things. You could paste insul-board over it, but it would get beaten up or eaten by beasties, or just wear off with the elements. So we need to cover the insulation and hold it onto the siding; we need this strapping. The other virtue of siding is that it covers up the container. Strong it may be; attractive it is not." He pointed out a big dint, a rusty patch, and a large stretch of scaling paint. "And there is the social stigma that some may lay on those who find that such a space is adequate to their needs. They are eco-friendly, you know, but some people might still demean them. Who needs others to make anyone's life harder?"

They moved around the side of the container they were then at and watched as wooden verticals were placed on the outside humps of the rippled side of the container. One man held it and drove a drill bit into the wood at waist height. When the bit hit steel, it slowed down and growled its way through the metal. Some were fascinated by the drillings that poured from the hole and then the way the man switched to the Power drill on his other hip to drive home a long screw. The younger children couldn't take their eyes off the big man himself with his long bushy beard. To them, he looked like a gigantic garden gnome.

"Let me show you inside," Dan continued. They walked to the end of the unit where the double doors stood wide open, and a brilliant work light illuminated the interior. Another man held strapping against the groove in the metal side. When an identical copy of the outside worker turned to greet them, the kids nearest jumped back.

"How did you get in here?" squeaked one child crowding into those behind her.

The giant smiled. "Get that all the time," he said in a soft lilt that seemed to come up from his shoes. He was moving forward, backing the children out of the container. He bent to pick up a new strap at his feet. "Excuse me," he said as he pressed it into a new recess just as the drilling started on the outside. He leaned a hip hard against the wood just as the pitch of the drill changed. There was a pause, and the sound of the screw came. The children closest saw the inside strip of wood pulled tight to the metal. Smoothly, the man picked up another piece of wood and placed it in a new groove, several from last, just as the sound started outside.

"How do you know where to put it?" one of the children asked.

"Well, I could tell you that my brother outside and I are telepathic, but that would be teasing you," Byron said softly. Actually, Dan there marked the places I have to put the wood with a chalk mark. He pointed to the small 'x' marks on the bottom of the wall where the studs needed to be placed. But as the children watched the next few studs get screwed in place and the harmonic coordination between the two men, they began to suspect the workers were really talking to each other somehow.

Again, the man excused himself to place wedging boards against each of the interior studs before joining his brother outside. Dan explained how the wedges held the wood inside tightly, while both, working from opposite ends, added the additional screws that would hold both outside and inside studs tightly in place from shoulder height down.

"They'll do the other side just as you saw them do that one," Dan explained "then go and get the ladder to do the two screws higher up. One holds the ladder, the other drills." Then they move to the next unit. Others are coming to do the insulation and add siding outside later.

"I think it is time for us to go," Jacob said. As they walked back, they saw other teams putting on insulating slabs and siding, as Dan had said.

"OK, you know your homework then," Jacob announced as they reached the doorway to their tower. "A list of the uses to which those containers are being put, for tomorrow." Simply by using the plural, he was telegraphing that they'd better suggest more than housing as a use. He turned to the cluster of older students. "You might be ready to offer insight into the problems you might have observed in implementing those uses and suggesting how the outcomes might be evaluated. Clear? Any questions?"

None.

"Bye, sir," chorused the group.

As they all waited for the elevators in the lobby, Jacob was surprised to see Detective Winters talking to Barak, the concierge. Both elevators arrived, and Jacob saw all his students aboard then joined them. The detective seemed to be checking his phone as if he was making an appointment.

*

"You're right, Brian," Jacob agreed the next day in class when the older student added the point of being a project that they all could work together on to the list on the board. Jacob then likened it to the Pythagorean School of so long ago. "How many used their multiplying skills to calculate the number of shipping containers in the lot?" Jacob had seen one group counting the units in the outside line and row.

A bunch of hands shot up to tell him the number.

"Excellent," when he got the correct answer. "Pythagoras also found that mathematics was in everything around him. To him, it was evidence of the magical fundamental that mathematics was a part of the essence of life.

"So any more uses that the containers serve besides

showing us that mathematics is a fundamental of life?"

He quickly reviewed the ideas on the board and read them out as he did. "'Places to live,' 'a way to learn skills,' 'helping each other by practicing good manners,' 'ways for people to show individuality,' 'recycling,' and 'team building' from Brian.

"Well done again. I congratulate you on your skill in seeing what things can mean," Jacob said.

He turned to the older pupils. "Did you spot problems in this strategy for doing all these wonderful things?"

"Dan, our guide, illustrated one problem," Victoria said. "He can't work like The Giants because he can't hold the tools."

"Leading us to accept …?"

"Individual differences." came the voice of Gretchen, another of his seniors. "Is everyone's work equal? That is the problem. Here is a situation that some could take advantage of. They do next to nothing, making others work harder, but they each get a place to live in when it's done."

"How could the problem Gretchen points out be resolved?" Jacob asked.

The chatter that followed described a token economy until someone said that the tokens were called money and everyone laughed. Brian's lone hand came up tentatively.

"I think it all depends on what you value. Gretchen said that some had to work harder because others don't, and that isn't fair that the slackers get something for nothing; or next to it. What if their skills are in something else? Dan can't do what the others do, but he makes sure that the work of the others is not wasted. He reads the plans which the others can't. What is the value of making somebody feel good or saving a life?"

Brian bit on his lip a moment and then began to tell how his teacher cut him out of a suicide vest that was set to explode almost two years before. The new students had not heard this story; the older ones knew it was the first time Brian had talked about the event from over a year ago. Jacob felt the tears welling up as he listened to the youngster talk about values far beyond his years.

"So I guess there are some things you can't give money for," Brian concluded. "Maybe all you can do is work harder and hope the slacker grows up when they see how you show you care."

The end-of-class bell chimed as Brian finished, but nobody moved. The first one who did slip out of her seat and ran over and gave Brian a big hug; everyone followed suit. Jacob just slumped against his desk, watching it all unfold while blinking hard. Brian was last to go, and as he did, he stopped and gave Jacob a big hug as well.

## 23

Jacob found that the time he didn't spend teaching was consumed with issues at the men's tower. It wasn't as though all the problems of the first batch of men were solved. But aside from Dexter and his motor scooter, there were no new challenges - just lots more of the old ones with the new members of the community.

He found the men who had reformed had almost become zealots in defending their new virtues. Abuse of drugs, booze, and gambling met with unflinching condemnation of others who practised them. There were just too many who might succumb to temptation if one of their numbers got away with collapse. So they were rigorous in keeping everyone on the straight and narrow. It wasn't the graciousness he had sought, but it was as good as was possible for now.

God help you if you found something and didn't return it to its owner. One of the new group members hadn't made it into the tower before he was spotted stealing tools. You'd have thought that it was apparent that it was a bad idea to try to steal from former thieves. Apparently, it wasn't.

The man really didn't think any of the old group had done what he had done, at least not as skillfully as he had.

And he had no idea of Pete's encyclopedic memory for numbers. The guy had claimed he'd brought the drill in from outside because the one Pete had given him was broken. Pete noted the serial number of the one in the guy's lunch box as he was about to leave one day and showed it was in his inventory. That guy was cashed out for work done on the spot and told not to return.

All the old guys had abandoned smoking, and they were pressuring the new arrivals to take the program that would make them smoke-free. Jacob had observed the unsubtle group pressures shared at the meal tables. "You smell like a bonfire," one had said. "What happened in your apartment?" or another's suggestion that he'd sit upwind when he moved to the other side of the table.

In spite of those moments, what inspired Jacob was the camaraderie and softness that accompanied their group gatherings. Best of all was the ukulele group and the developing male choir. There were only about twenty in the choir now, but a few more came forward to join every couple of weeks. They needed more tenors.

The choir's recruitment song, which got sung almost weekly at supper time, was ***All God's Creatures Got a Place in the Choir***. Almost all the men now knew the song and joined in clapping, even if they didn't follow the choir off to rehearsal. Gary and Thumb accompanied the group. They mentioned that they needed someone to play bass and another to do the fiddle. "Do we have any fiddlers - no not that kind - the violin types," was the invitation one night. A couple confessed to learning the violin in childhood, but as of yet, nobody had come forward to take the slot. Jacob wondered if he could get anybody from the local orchestra to become a part of the Vagabonds, as the ukulele types called themselves. It was a good start.

One of the enduring problems was hoarding. Harold became the community archivist, and that at least justified his collecting of newspapers for a short term, but Bruce or TD still had to tell him that Pete was coming by the next day to take the stuff to the recycler. Maybe it was partly due to his medications, or perhaps it was the security of the place - it didn't matter. He was becoming less anxious about seeing all that good stuff disappear. And he was becoming adept enough at finding information on his computer that he was able to help others look for jobs, best deals, and best of all, current fashion trends. The guys couldn't stop laughing over that.

Jacob hoped that Harold's example and supportive effort from new friends would have the same effect on the other guys who couldn't throw anything away. It was those with drug addictions that kept Jacob awake at night. Anyone addicted to some drug who signed up had to get a clean pass from the rehab program first. Then they could join the work team and work with others who had made it, or who never had the problem. If the guy relapsed, the group was confrontational.

"Do you think it's our job to keep you on a habit here?" one had been asked when he was spotted shooting up.

"Did you join us just for a safe place to do your drugs? Well, think again. We're in the business of keeping a whole bunch of others in safe housing. That's at risk if we become known as some sort of drug hi-rise. So you get one more chance. If you don't like us, just say so. We can take rejection. We've written the book on it. You can be out of here now - like right now. But if you expect to join us, you must become bigger than you are now. We'll help you do that."

"But someone slipped it into my insulin," the delinquent had sputtered.

The group met that with a string of obscenities that Jacob felt he didn't need to hear. He'd left as they were laying down the law to the man. Three days later, the guy had been found dead.

"Drug overdose," was the word from the paramedics who saw the guys saw cleaning up.

"Suicide" was the way it was reported at supper.

"You can't fix stupid," Jacob had heard from the group that he'd accompanied down in the elevator.

Jacob walked home wondering if 'helping with grace' could fix stupid and arrived home discouraged. It was a depressing prelude to the call that caught him the next day as he left his class.

*

"It's Owen," the voice said when Jacob got to the call as he walked from his classroom. The message had just ended. "Rajik is my neighbour. He needs your help right away."

Jacob called Owen back as he was crossing the parking lot. "You called about Rajik."

"Yeah. He's having a bad day with his depression after he found one of his buddies from under the bridge was dead."

"Was the man the one in our community? The guy they were talking about at supper?"

"No. This guy stayed out. It seems Rakik found the guy under the bridge yesterday."

"I'll be there in a moment; I'm coming in the door from the parking lot as we speak. Are you at his place?"

"We're at the window overlooking the creek on our floor, right outside his door."

The walkway was deserted except for the two men leaning on the railing, looking out the window.

"Afternoon, guys," he called as he came up. Owen turned; Rajik did not.

"Can you tell me what happened?" Jacob asked quietly.

There was a silence as Rajik seemed to be struggling back to awareness. "I went down to see him yesterday. The doc said it might be helpful to talk to old friends to tell them how well I'm doing. Everybody here knows I'm getting better. So I went to see if Tank was still under the bridge. He didn't want to come - "He didn't want to sleep in a box," he said. It was a nice day. I just went to see if he was there." Rajik was starting to breathe more quickly.

"So there was nobody around, but Tank seemed to be sleeping where he usually does - up on the slope near the wall under the bridge. Looked like he was taking a nap. It was afternoon. And then I got there. I called him--" He couldn't go on.

"Tank was dead," Owen said, "and he had been for a while. He'd been chewed on. It was a bad scene."

"What did you do, Rajik? It must have been a horrible shock."

"I just sat down. I didn't know what to do. I waited for him to wake up. I tapped his boot. Something ran out from under his coat. It was dark then, and I was getting cold. I just came home and went to bed."

"I was doing night shift last night, so I wasn't here at supper; I asked when Rajik didn't show for breakfast. So I came to get him, and that's when I found out. I made the call to the police."

"Did he talk to Bruce?"

"Yeah, and Bruce gave him something extra; he has an appointment tomorrow with the doctor."

"Do the rest of the guys know?"

"The news is going around now."

Jacob laid a hand on Rajik's arm where it rested on the railing. "I'm really sorry, Rajik. It is a hard thing to lose a friend." Jacob's thoughts went back to the moment, years ago now, when his own wife died and the emptiness he felt.

"He was a bit of a grouch most of the time, but he looked out for me, brought me a meal now and again. Had a terrible time with booze. I remember he talked about dying once, how he thought it would be bad to die alone. I think he must have died in his sleep from the way I saw him."

"The police ask for a statement yet?" Jacob asked.

"They don't know Rajik found him. I just left a message on their anonymous line."

"Do you know where he came from, Rajik? Maybe his name?"

"I thought he said he was First Nation sometime. Never knew him by any other name but Tank."

"You know, I feel like I'm a fly on that window." He looked up at the sky. "I'm watching this guy who feels so bad, and that person is me. I think I feel bad, but I just don't give a damn. How can that be?"

"It's medicine talking," Jacob said. "That's what Tank said. He was always talking about medicine but not like it was pills and stuff, but a way to feel, a spirit thing. I never understood him, and it made him feel bad that he couldn't share what he meant. But when I think of him now and I feel so empty and..." He waved a hand aimlessly.

Everyone slouched on the railing, looking out the window at the creek below. The bridge where Tank had died was just at the edge of their view.

"And he died right there," Rajik said, looking down. "He could have joined us here. Why didn't he?" They just stared out as the light faded.

"The others will be gathering upstairs soon. Why don't we go up there and talk about him?" Jacob suggested.

The guys were sincere in their sorrow about Tank's passing. They all had stared down that tunnel. Of course, they wanted to know how he died, and nobody knew. "He wasn't into drugs unless he picked it up lately." They went on to talk about the times they had shared and laughed at the simple pleasures.

While that was going on, Jacob talked to Bruce about keeping an eye on Rajik and then lamenting another death within their group - well within the circle they travelled.

"Jake, you know as well as I do that these guys are closer to it than those you had in your church. They've been beaten up by life, and they've piled up lots of problems that end in only one way."

"Doesn't make it any easier."

"Got that right." After he left the penthouse wake, Jacob called the private number of Detective Winters to offer the little information he had about the dead vagrant. Maybe he had ways to find out where he came from. Someone would surely like to know he had died.

24

"What's that doing there?" Jacob asked when he saw the Scotch thistle blossoming proudly in The Scotsmen's planter box. You know it's a noxious weed." They must have brought it into the tower in a pot where the seed was planted back in the spring. As soon a Jacob saw the prickly bristles, they made his skin itch. In his youth, a garden hoe was what you reached for as soon as you saw one. If they got started in your garden, tending veggies became even more of a chore.

"Onopordum acanthium L., Family Compositae," said Byron with pride. "Carl Linnaeus named it, you know. That's why his initial is at the end." He continued to fill an envelope with seeds.

"Did you ever hear the story about how the national flowers came to be?" Blake asked when Jacob didn't move on.

Jacob had to turn around and look away from the enormous bushy plant that towered into the air. It was overhead high in its own pot and partway up the vertical garden. Clusters of vivid purple flowers burst from the stem—whispy fluff from seeds about to drift away stuck out of maturing flower clumps. Byron folded the envelope closed and carefully slid it into his pocket.

"Well, there was an auction," Byron began, "to decide which nations should have the right to attach which flower to their name. Mother told us so," he said in a broad brogue. "It seems the Scots got the message late."

"It took one of the custodians in the hall where the event was to happen a while to figure out what the diplomat was trying to say, but eventually he did and said, "M'lord was too late. The event was all over," Blake butted in.

"Now, this was a junior diplomat, and if he returned to the embassy empty-handed, he could expect his career to end immediately. He managed to get the caretaker to relate the event so that at least he could tell his boss the story of what had happened even though he'd been late and missed it all." Byron waved him on.

"The British pushed the bidding on the rose, you know. They had so much money; there was no doubt about who was going to get it. But the other guys kept raising the ante to make the Brits go just a little further. Everyone quite enjoyed tweaking the lion's tail."

Byron picked up the tale in what became tag-team storytelling. "The French got the lily, although the Italians were pretty ticked. When they'd missed the rose, they wanted the lily too, but they settled for the poppy. A bunch of the delegation thought that was a bad idea and insisted a bid be placed for the violet. They were arguing last I saw them."

"What did the Welsh get?" the diplomat asked.

"Ooo, they came on strong for the daffodil. The Brits decided to let them have it despite the grief they'd given them over the rose bidding."

"And the Irish?"

Blake took his turn. "Poor as dirt they are, I don't think they even got a flower at all. All they took home was a pot of green stuff."

"Well, the diplomat was pretty down," Byron continued. "He had nothing to take back as the symbol of his negotiating skill, and the rest wasn't much of a story. He cast his eyes around the hall, empty except for the cleaners and a pile of debris they had swept up. But out of that heap peaked a lovely cluster of purple flowers. The diplomat picked up the pot and avoided the prickly leaves.

"So what's this one? Who bid on it?"

"The cleaner was amazed at the man's ignorance. "You don't want that one, for heaven's sake. It's a weed!"

But the Scot's eyes lit up immediately. "So I presume it's free?" he confirmed with a lilt.

Both the Smythe brothers spread their arms wide as though worshiping the thistle.

"It's a good story, guys," Jacob complimented, "and you tell it well, but you should take photos and then cut it down before it hurts somebody. You know, as soon as it gets a complaint, it will face termination. They might even cancel your planter privileges. You know what happened to those who planted marijuana." That made them both laugh. A couple of the guys had decided a practical joke was in order to suggest that some of the new planters be seeded with a selection of native wildflowers. It was quite some time before the weed was discovered. They had convinced the planter that it was buttercup until the plant's height gave it away.

"Alright, laddie," Blake said with a laugh. The plant's purpose had been fulfilled. It had given them enough seeds for another generation and gotten the proper response from the high-priced help. "We'll take it along." The heavy sleeves on his jacket protected his hands as he hoisted the pot from the stand. Both were laughing amiably as they walked off together.

*

Detective Winters had asked Jacob to join him as they walked the grounds of the tower following his call about Tank's death. He wanted to acknowledge Jacob's helping with the investigation of the dead vagrant under the bridge. It was the tip they needed to narrow the search. They'd found kin who had claimed the body.

"The guy died of natural causes. The autopsy said

though it was a toss-up if it was liver failure or a heart problem that did him in," Winters summarized. Another sad story. "But I'll tell you something that really surprised me. The man died with two hundred dollar bills in his pocket."

That brought Jacob up short. "Why does anyone die with that much money sleeping on the ground under a bridge."

"That was only part of the surprise," Winters added. Jacob waited.

"Do you recall the night I met you and I met your buddies coming out of work? They had a couple of lunch coolers. One was named TD, as I recall. He handed it to me to look into. It had a lot of money in it. Do you remember the day?"

"I recall that night. Yeah," agreed Jacob.

"Well, we put the lunch bucket back in place after we noted the serial numbers on the bills and marked them with some special dye we have that is invisible. I thought it was odd at the time that some of those bills were marked with a three-digit code. The numbers were not sequential, but all those bills were placed in the order of the numbers written on them. It was just one of the coincidences that leap out in my life."

Jacob waited. He was sure there was another shoe to drop.

"We found two hundred dollar bills in the vagrant's pocket. You'd have to think that was another amazing coincidence, wouldn't you? And further, the bills on the body had a three-digit number in the margins. The numbers were the same as the two on the ones in that cooler that TD gave us, but we marked them with invisible ink. The ones on the body didn't have our ink marker."

"So it looks like whatever the numbers meant was some sort of code and that the business for which the code was needed, continued. You found it once when TD gave you that cooler, and there was a second similar event that needed the same number after that one. Have I got that right?"

Winters nodded.

Jacob didn't know what to say, so he just shut up. He had expected to talk about the positive changes since the previous spring. It wasn't working out that way.

Winters revealed the other reason he'd come over. It was about a workman named Zid.

"After enquiries, we thought we had enough to convince a judge to issue a search warrant, did so, and went to the address we had. Mr. Zid was not there. He had gone to work and not come home, the landlord explained. When the rent was not paid for a month, he'd called a dumpster and thrown the few things in the apartment out."

Winters continued with his follow-up at the worksite and found a report that said Austin Zid was believed to have gone home with a gastric complaint in mid-afternoon. He had not checked out at the work site, possibly because of his illness, the report concluded. But he had not arrived home.

"Well, I don't know what to say," Jacob said. They were watching a friend that had come with Detective Winters walkabout with the man's dog on a long leash.

When the detective said nothing, Jacob felt obliged to restart the conversation.

"Nice dog," he complimented.

"His name is Scout."

"What kind is he?"

"He's a cadaver dog. That's the dog's vocation, not the breed," Winters elaborated. It wasn't what Jacob had expected.

"What?! What is he doing here?"

"I've run out of ideas, so it's my last thought," Winters explained. "We'll know soon enough if Mr. Zid is still here. It's the last box to fill before I close the file."

The silence stretched out longer.

"How does a cadaver dog tell anyone that there is a body somewhere?"

"It is trained to make some sort of display when it finds the smell of a dead body."

They watched as the man and dog crisscrossed the space, gradually shortening the run until the dog stopped and laid down with his nose against the wall of the building.

"What sort of display does Scout show?" Jacob asked.

"He lies down."

Both were quietly watching as the handler rewarded the dog. "Like that?" Jacob asked with rising anxiety.

"Yep."

25

The inquest concluded that Austin Zid had died by accident from striking a sharp concrete corner. There was abundant evidence to show he had not been feeling well shortly before his death. It was reasonable to surmise that he had fainted after a significant bowel movement following standing up, just after he had exited from the toilet. The inquest concluded further that he had fallen into the trench that was about to be filled, striking his head as he fell on a concrete ledge of the wall. The man died almost instantly, and the trench was filled without his body being discovered. No blame was assigned to the workers involved.

Jacob had gotten a release from his classes to attend all the proceedings. The death had happened on their site, after all. He endured the process, looked at all the photographs, listened to details that he blamed for his poor sleep in the weeks that followed. But he had forced himself to pay strict attention to the detailed examination of the wound, the granular inclusions identical to the composition of the foundation wall, the list of broken bones and blood vessels. Those minutiae had not kept him awake then, so why the horrible dreams now?

It was as he jolted from another nightmare that he realized that it was not the decayed corpse or the medical progression towards death following the fatal fall that brought him suddenly to his senses. Winston no longer shared the house; he had his own place in the tower. Jacob had nobody to talk to. He shuffled into the bathroom and stood looking at himself in the mirror. He laid his hand along the line of the fracture that had done Mr. Zid in - from the crown of his head, down across the right temple to the broken cheekbones on that side. He imagined the bathtub was the ditch beside the concrete wall, and he stepped towards it as though he was falling. He pretended the rough concrete reached out, and he scrubbed it as he imagined the fall.

No. He mentally backed up. He'd have to topple almost entirely to the bottom to have enough speed to do the damage that was found on the skull. But the photographs showed no such sharp ledge at that depth that could have smashed the head. There was one higher up. He had to have hit it in mid-fall.

But that wasn't the problem, he realized. It was that if Zid had fallen in the way that produced those injuries from hitting projections on the wall, the corpse's head would have been facing the other way. The body was found completely turned around. If the body had fallen into the ground as it was found, the injuries should have been on the left side of the skull, not the right. But there was no concrete obstacle on the body's right, Just dirt.

He had to sit down; he felt so faint. He thudded onto the edge of the tub and leaned forward to get some blood into his head. He put a hand out to the toilet seat to steady himself from toppling too far forward and waited till he recovered. When he sat back up, his skin felt clammy.

He staggered carefully back to his bedroom and punched the speed dial.

"Hello?" came the sleepy reply.

"Bruce, It's Jacob. I know it's the middle of the night, but could you come over here right now?"

"What's wrong?"

"I feel faint, my skin is clammy, and I want to throw…"

"Christ, call 9--," Bruce interrupted.

"No. NO-- No, please don't do that. It is something else. Can you come over right away? I won't be dead when you get here."

"I'm on my way. I can bike it in less than ten. Keep talking to me, will you?"

"I'm going to the front door to open it. It will be ajar when you get here. I'll be in the living room."

\*

When Bruce rushed in, Jacob was sitting with the coroner's report in his lap. "Look at this," he said, holding out the photograph of the decayed body in the bottom of the trench.

Bruce closed his eyes a moment then opened them. "OK. This is Zid?"

"Right." Jacob described the wall. Bruce nodded in recognition.

"And that is the ledge the guy's head hit that killed him?" Bruce pointed at the photo.

"Yeah. Now come with me to the bathroom, and I'll pretend to fall into the tub as though it was this trench." He brought the photos and lined up as though would fall and land in the pictured position.

"Right," agreed Bruce.

"OK. In slo-mo, I'm going to pretend to fall as if I've fainted. Over I go, head hits the ledge. Bash, I'm dead, and then I land at the bottom. Right?"

"Right. Now, look at the photo."

"Yeah, but if that is correct, I should have smashed the left side of my head, which was bashed in in the photo."

"The right. So that means that your fall wasn't the way Zid did it."

"So show me how he fell."

Bruce stood there turning his head, looking into the tub and back at the photo.

"OK, here's how it happened. He fell backwards, not forwards, struck his head, and the impact flipped him over onto his face."

"Through more than a three-quarter roll?"

Bruce was quiet. "Well, he might not have been dead at the moment he hit the ground. He could have been conscious for a moment and rolled over before he succumbed. I mean, there was no recovering from that wound. A reflexive spasm could have rolled the body."

"How likely is that?"

"I can tell you that bodies do peculiar things in the throes of death."

"Could have he been injured before he fell in?"

"The man didn't walk around after hitting his head like that and then falling in. That impact happened within a few feet of where he came to lie. The ledge was most likely the impact edge."

"The blood detail tells me the body did not move after initial impact with the ground." He paused for a moment. "And any other alternative your suggesting would have to be the most bizarre suicide I can imagine or murder with a piece of concrete from the foundation."

"Show me how."

Bruce looked at the photos carefully. He muttered to himself as he gyrated around as he worked out how an intentional plunge into the trench with the head striking the ledge and then the complete roll of the body could work. And then he showed how an overhead downward swing with a chunk of concrete could do the injury and then the body could have been turned as it fell to come to lie as it was in the picture. "But that would mean… I don't think those are reasonable scenarios."

"I wish you had said that with more enthusiasm," Jacob said. "Thanks, I'm sorry to get you up. All I could think of was one alternative, and I don't know what I would do if my nightmare was what really happened."

"So I can go home now?"

Jacob patted Bruce's arm as he showed him out. "Thanks again."

He watched as Bruce put on his helmet and cycled away in the pre-dawn grey.

"OK," he thought to himself. "Bruce thinks it's pretty unlikely TD clobbered Zid with a chunk of concrete." He was reflecting back on the moment he'd seen TD pass money to the homeless man - that was months ago. The guy could have come by the marked money a whole bunch of ways. He didn't have to have gotten it from TD - but it was the most direct connection to have come from that route. Did TD pick up the lunch bucket and keep the money? Maybe he cleaned the cash out of the lunch cooler and left it. It would have been sensible to do if you knew the man was not coming to pick it up himself. But how would he know that? That was what was gnawing at him.

# 26

Spring was well advanced; the sun shone more than half the day. The group that was contracting themselves out as set builders had managed to impress people in the few amateur theatres with whom they had worked, encouraging them to try for larger venues. They had found an agent who was going to represent them to movie companies, both for the auditorium itself and any set they could build for it. The agent was surprised to find out about the panoramic view from the penthouse and asked if it might be advertised for movie shoots. There seemed to be no opposition to that pending the details of the precise needs of the company. So that was chugging along under TD's management.

TD's constant attention to the men who worked under him in the workshop seemed to lift them off the ground. He had guys using equipment that others wouldn't dare let them use. He had guys who seemed unable to follow two consecutive instructions producing products for the stage sets they were building that had others asking where they came from. The man had a talent for giving men jobs that they could do and help those guys feel proud of the way they did it. A born leader, that man.

TD was hosting a small party at his place to celebrate their most recent contract - what else could they have in a house like his? It was Jacob, Maggie, and Bruce. Winston was invited because he ran the cafeteria and brought food, Jacob thought. And he got a couple of chairs from the cafeteria tables. The lounge chairs just wouldn't fit. Though it was a cozy group in the space, the picture window at one end and the mega TV screen with the view of the skyline helped to dispel the claustrophobic quality.

"Well done," Maggie said with a raised glass, and everyone followed suit. To have nailed that contract with the movie producer moves you into the big leagues. That will give you work for the next year, right?"

TD nodded. "We seem to work well with the director and the set designer. We can take an idea and implement it in much less time than their previous builders. I guess as long as we can compete, we keep the job. But it is gratifying to see the ink on that paper." He waved the contract. "And the chuckle is that the director asked the Smythe brothers to come for a screen test. They couldn't stop laughing. It seems they'll be playing one role, but if they are in different costumes, the shooting schedule can be shortened - not much, but these movie moguls count pennies."

They all laughed at the pair who played games with everyone by claiming that instructions were given to their brother, not them, so that whoever it was had to repeat himself. "You know, one of the guys thought he had their number. He managed to get one of them and slip a dot on the back of his coveralls. Took them no time at all to add a second dot to the other guy's uniform."

"Were they looking for any others as extras? You know, or people in a crowd, that sort of thing?" asked Winston.

"You want to be a movie star - name in lights?" TD joked. "Sure. He gave me a card."

He pulled a worn leather wallet from his rear pocket. It was hanging by a chain attached to his belt. The jingling clink caught Jacob's attention, and he looked over. TD opened the wallet and sorted out the business card from his health card and driver's license, some small bills.

"Here it is," he said, passing it across to Winston. He reached forward, and as he did, the wallet opened to show money in the pocket behind the other cards. Jacob's stared at what he saw. It wasn't the colourful card with the director's name and contact numbers that was crossing the space to Winston that startled him. Jacob saw the brownish edge and number that declared it was a hundred dollar bill in the moment. The shiny hologram of Sir Robert Borden looked back at him for an instant. And on the edge of the bill, right beside the value, was written a number - a three-digit number - 664 - in black ink. TD held the wallet open a moment for Jacob to stare at the bill in disbelief while TD directed Winston to turn the card to the number on the back. Jacob looked up in anguish. Bruce was looking at him with concern and followed Jacob's wide-eyed, open-mouthed gaze.

*Had he said anything?* Jacob wondered. It didn't

matter. He suddenly felt like he was going to faint. There were prickles of bright light he hadn't noticed dancing in the air. The edge of his field of view was black and closing in.

"Put your head down," Bruce said in his ear, and a firm hand forced his face between his knees.

Winston had copied the details from the business card into his own phone and handed the card back. Jacob's commotion turned everyone in his direction. When he finally struggled back to uprightness, the billfold had disappeared, and everyone was staring at him.

"What happened?" demanded Maggie from the other side of the circle.

Jacob tried to say something but the words wouldn't come.

"I think he just felt faint," Bruce interjected. "Probably past his bedtime."

"Jacob," Maggie commanded. "Look at me. What's wrong?"

He shook his head and wiped a hand across his eyes. "I… I suddenly felt dizzy. I guess I shouldn't have finished the bottom of that beer," he stammered. He shook his head again. "I feel alright now, just a bit embarrassed." He drew a big breath and sent a wan smile around the group.

Maggie flashed a look at Bruce, whose hand on

Jacob's wrist. He nodded and took back his hand. "Well, your colour is coming back," Maggie observed. "Maybe it's time we got you home."

"I'll give him a ride on my bike," offered Bruce, and everyone laughed.

"I think he's earned a taxi," Maggie said. "Will you go with him and stay overnight, Bruce? I just want to be sure he's OK."

Jacob stood a bit unsteadily and took a few breaths. "I think that is probably a good idea. Sorry to break up the party."

"No problem," TD replied. "The big announcement was the reason, and we all enjoyed the chance to share it. It was time to end, anyways."

Jacob looked at him with a feeling of incomprehension. He knew the face; the voice sounded familiar, but he felt he was looking at a stranger. "*And why was there a fine mist of sweat along his hairline?*" Jacob wondered.

Still feeling a bit queasy, he allowed strong hands to turn him towards the door. The coolness of the hallway felt good. By the time they got to the lobby door, the taxi was there, and Maggie paid for it in advance. Jacob's stomach felt much better. His step was decisive. He protested that he was alright and could make his way home - to no avail. He was bundled into the excessively floral confines of the car, Bruce bumped in beside him, and they were off.

They drove in silence to Jacob's house. When they were inside, Bruce asked, "Want to tell me what you saw in TD's wallet that freaked you out?"

Jacob flopped into his chair as Bruce took the corner of the couch opposite.

"I told you about my nightmares with the body. You told me that I was unreasonable to suspect TD might have clobbered Zid and dumped him. I got that. I was being… crazy. I didn't tell you the other pieces that were on my puzzle board." He sighed deeply.

"The night we talked to those guys under the bridge, just before we left, I saw TD give Tank some money. When I was talking to Detective Winters just before they found Zid's body, he told me that they found two hundred dollar bills in the man's pocket. That alone seemed odd, but he went on to say that both bills had three-digit numbers written on them in ink. And those numbers were two of the numbers on bills that the police removed from those coolers. Remember when TD handed them over to the cops at the pub across the street?" Bruce nodded.

"Well, the police marked those bills in the cooler with some sort of invisible stuff. The bills on Tank had no such mark. But you'd have to admit the coming across two more bills of the same value with similar numbers on them is too much of a coincidence."

Jacob looked down and drew another breath. "Anyways, what I saw in TD's wallet tonight was another hundred dollar bill, and in the margin was a three-digit number in ink. The number was 664. So it suggests that TD gave Tank the bills and that TD has at least one more, and all these numbered bills somehow connect to Zid, but after the cops got the cooler and set up the sting." Bruce was sitting impassively, letting Jacob talk.

"The way this could be interpreted is that whatever scam Zid was running continued, and suddenly Zid disappears and is later found dead. AND, TD winds up with the money the man had collected. So how do you connect those dots?"

They both sat quietly until Bruce suggested, "I think we both need to go to bed and get some sleep. He leaned over and untied his boots and set them neatly beside the couch. Then he leaned over and pulled open the blanket that was folded on the other end. "And I'll sleep here. See you in the morning. Call me if you need me."

He pulled a cushion from under his arm, tossed it to the opposite end, and stretched out under the blanket.

Jacob just looked at him. "How did he do that?" he wondered. Bruce was asleep before Jacob got out of his chair.

*

Jacob answered Maggie's request for a chat the next day after class. He was never sure when he got an invitation to the boss's office at the end of the day. Was this serious and so needed a lot of time? Or trivial - the last thing that needed to be done before going home?

He knocked on Maggie's office door, which sat ajar. Zorina, Maggie's secretary, was already gone. "Come in, Jacob," she called before she saw him.

He signed inwardly when she waved him to the couch. If this was going to be the other type of meeting, she'd have left him standing or invited him to the hard wooden chair kept along the wall for the purpose.

As he made his way across the room, he felt he was being scrutinized. Maggie had been a head nurse in her pre-heiress life, and she'd lost none of her assessment skills. "You look like you're feeling better. Glad to see it. I'm going to have my usual. Can I get you one too?"

"Yes, please. Maybe one finger, lots of ice."

While the ice rattled into glasses, he looked around the room. A coat hook and large garment covered the dint in the door resulting from her previously hurling a heavy ashtray at him. He wondered if it was a permanent part of the decor now. The smell of fruit cake made him turn. She took a sliver before she set down the well-filled plate on the table.

"Iechyd da," he responded to Maggie's "Cheers."

"I'll presume that is a greeting from one of the guys."

"Yes - a Welshman."

"I wanted to talk to you about how well you've moved the project along," Maggie began without further preamble. "You got the group going. You doubled the population with impressive speed and success. I hear nothing but good things from the men when I meet them. You…"

"Please stop. I have not done that much at all. Any success has been due to the guys themselves or people like Bruce, Hat, Gary, Winston… and TD. They are the ones who made things happen. I don't know what I did that was even close to what those men did."

"You created the vision, and you kept it in front of them all. You've inspired them to create something unique. That is what leaders do, Jacob."

"Didn't know that. I just thought that was being a human."

"Well, I wish I'd had more like you along my way. But you scared me last night, and it brings up a detail of leadership that none of us who do the job want to talk much about. We each must find our replacement. You belong to the demographic for whom changes are frequently connected to bad events. They come unannounced, and they are usually serious. So what I'd like you to start to think about is who could replace you."

She immediately saw his wrinkled brow and deep breath. "I'm not trying to force you out. I want you to stay on doing what you're doing as long as you want. It's just that you scared everyone in the room last night, and it made us all realize we'd be in trouble without you. So this is a job to put on your back burner. The group will continue if you find someone to do what you do."

"I hear you. I'm glad you brought it up, actually, because I've found myself in a position I've never had before, and I honestly don't know what to do. When you ask me to think of someone who could do whatever it is you think I do, the name that pops into my mind is Pete."

"You mean the beer can guy? I didn't think he said even a sentence a week."

"Pete has an encyclopedic knowledge of everything about this building. If it has a serial number, he knows it. He can tell you when every wall and window was installed. He knows every man's birthday and the day they got out of jail or rehab. I don't think he knows their social insurance numbers, but that is only because nobody asked him to remember them. He's a no-nonsense guy, and everybody would sooner do what he tells them is right than argue with him because everyone knows he will win. He simply outlasts everyone. So, logic and information are his strong suits. Emotional issues are not. But he's making headway there too. Anyway, that's the name that popped up as soon as you asked me as to who could take over."

"How about the others? We need someone to take over for Bruce. I think the group needs someone like him to provide on-site medical aid as he does."

"I could ask him who he'd suggest."

"Winston is another who should have an understudy."

Jacob could feel himself growing tense as the name he didn't want to talk about approached.

"I think Winston could best suggest how or who we might get as a backup that could do his job. We'd have to promote him, give him a bigger salary - commensurate with his additional responsibilities as we'd have to do with the others." He tossed down the remnants of his drink and set his glass down too hard. He snatched the last piece of fruitcake from the plate and bolted it in one bite without even thinking. He hunched forward and closed his eyes, waiting for the next question.

Maggie said nothing. She stood and collected their drinks and the cake plate and returned them to the sideboard. When she returned, she sat on the edge of her chair and reached across the coffee table to touch his shoulder. Jacob broke down.

Nobody had touched him like that since his wife, but she was dead for years now. She managed to convey such wholehearted concern and love in such a simple act. He could not stop sobbing.

"Tell me, Jacob," Maggie said. They were the very words his wife had said so long ago. He stopped weeping and slumped away from the touch, back into the couch and wiped the tears from his face. "I can do no right here. Whatever I do, is damned. How can I tell you?"

"Tell me, Jacob. It is right to do so." And he did.

The daylight fell into dusk, then darkness. He talked on, examining every alternative and still reaching the same conclusion. "I believe, as surely as I'm sitting here, that TD must have killed Zid. If I pretend he didn't, I must give up my belief in the sanctity of all life. If I pass along the tidbits that link the parts of the puzzle and betray a friend, how can I ever ask friendship of any other?"

They sat in the dimness; only street light from below penetrated the gloom for some time until Maggie stood and started to tour the office, turning on lights. "It is so typical of people with religious training to see things in single alternatives. You surprise me, Jacob, that in all the liberation theology I've heard from you since I met you, that you still fall back on 'either-or' simplicity. I can think of several other facets to this situation. I'll give you the top of the list. And..." with reference to another distant day, she added, "you'll notice I picked up all the heavy objects before I state the obvious."

That brought a reluctant chuckle from Jacob.

"The third alternative to your supposed dilemma is this." She paused for dramatic effect. "You're wrong - just plain wrong! You started with bad premises; you made coincidence into cause in your own mind. You spun castles in the air out of imagination. If I challenge a single fact that you supposedly claim, you'll go back to rationalizing your wrongness with more and more circular arguments that will leave you even more convinced of your truth. Not long ago, you confronted me with an awful truth. I was wrong, but I simply would not hear it." She strode to the office door and removed the coat. "I left this dint as a daily reminder that I can't afford the luxury of omniscient knowledge. You told me facts I didn't want to hear, but you were right." She had replaced her coat and moved back to her chair.

"And now the shoe is on the other foot. The facts are that an inquest found Zid died of a blow to the head suffered by a fall into that trench. Bruce has tried to interpret what you saw as a wrong conclusion. But no. You had a fixation that would not let you see the obvious. Do you think all those forensic people who worked on the case didn't see that? How dumb do you think they are?"

"You have leapt to the conclusion that TD handed over those bills to Tank. "How much of a leap of faith do you want? That is worthy of Superman. I could make up a dozen scenarios as likely as that one. And then you link a bill with numbers on it in TD's wallet to the same string of unlikely connections. You're like the tradesman with only a hammer. Everything is a nail."

"So you think I'm obsessive?"

"You hit the top symptoms. But you are not alone in your misery. In my other life as a nurse, I dealt with stories like this almost daily. You have come to a conclusion that flies in the face of so much hard evidence, but you cannot give it up. It is the measure of how strongly we believe in ourselves."

"I'm telling you, you don't have to drop down that spiral. Say 'Stop.' And change the channel."

Jacob had gotten up to stare into the twinkling darkness.

"And just to put a fine point on it. When you get to be a leader, as you reluctantly are, here is another thing they might not have taught you at Divinity College. It's not just about you! You have corporate duties to discharge. You are called upon to weigh the good of the many against that of the few. So I suggest you seek solace in doing what hasn't been accomplished as well as… well, you tell me. You're the historian."

Maggie let that sink in a moment, then continued softly. "And here is the hardest part of all, Jacob. Are you still listening?" Jacob nodded without turning around.

"The absolutes you were taught to seek in the church don't exist in the real world. We live in a life of ambiguity and uncertainty. You will do the best you can based on all you know and experience. But it is arrogant in the extreme to imagine that today's right is eternally so. You have given the guidance of giving and accepting help with grace. It works. Your men buy into that. It is a good thing now, and maybe forever, but you will never know, nor should you expect to. The test of your faith in humanity will be if you ever find that you were wrong - about anything you thought was important. Will you have the strength to forgive yourself or anyone else who fails your standard?"

It was quiet for a while.

Maggie broke the silence by getting up and opening a cupboard in the sideboard. She removed a heavy glass ashtray and set it on her desk behind where Jacob still stood looking out the window.

"And here's the mate to the one I threw at you. Just give me a head start."

Jacob turned at that and saw her looking at him. He made a sudden move towards the object and saw a flash of panic in her eyes. It was what at least a few of the guys would have done, and he'd have reacted just as she did. He must be learning something. Jacob stepped back, smiling, then laughing with relief. She was laughing too.

"Please put it away for another day," Jacob suggested. "I suddenly feel hungry. Is the cafeteria still open?"

"Not likely. Look at the time."

Maggie pulled out her phone and hit a speed dial number. "Pour us another round," she directed Jacob and turned back to the phone. When she sat down, she said, "ham and cheese on rye coming in fifteen along with apple crisp and ice cream. Carafe of decaf on the side."

"How do you do that?" Jacob asked.

"I work late a lot and have a secret source. It is another leadership skill."

"Well, I'm not going to learn to work late, so I won't

need a secret source. That's a higher leadership skill. Sláinte." He lifted his drink.

"Cheers," she replied.

"Hmmm."

## 27

"It's come down from great heights that I'm supposed to have a designate to take over in case I die," said TD to Dan. They had just finished going over the drawings and the artist's rendition of the plans for the movie set that they had to create. "Want the job?"

"Is this because of Jake's 'spell' the other night?"

"You heard about that?"

"Duh."

"Probably, anyway, so you want the job?"

"And that job is?"

"Running the shop, looking for new jobs, keeping the guys happy."

"Isn't that what we all do?"

"Yeah, but if the boss thinks something is wrong or needs something new, there has to be someone she talks to. Having a group meeting isn't the way they do things. Right now, that someone is me, but if I wasn't here, it could be you."

"You planning on dying?"

"Stop making this hard. No, I'm not planning on dying. I just need to pass along a name. I think you'd be the best one to do the job, but if it isn't yours, it will be someone else's who doesn't have your talents, and you'd have to follow what they say."

"Well, since you put it that way, OK, I'll accept with grace." He bowed theatrically. "Wish I'd brought my cape so I could do that bow the way they did it in the last movie. And speaking of movies, I know you thought we'd finished the review, but I just realized while you were talking that these plans don't match the artist's concept."

With the hand that had been so badly crushed years earlier, he pushed the roll of blueprints aside to find the watercolour drawing below. "See the steps that lead to this platform in the library. I read the script for this scene, and the action goes on down here on the lower level, and then the female lead runs up these steps and out that door."

"So?"

"Well, when she exits through that door," he lifted and pulled the blueprint back, and his good hand pointed to the doorway, "she would find herself four feet above the off-stage floor and in free-fall. There are no stairs or a platform for her to exit onto."

"Is that a dangling participle you ended with?" TD asked.

Dan ignored the jibe. "No, it's a dangling movie star."

"See, that is why I want you to do this job. How many people would have missed that? So you'll do it?"

"Fix my grammar? Or the missing platform?" Dan was getting some of his own back.

"The job," TD said in exasperation and with a twinge of pleading in his voice.

"Yeah. OK." Dan smiled, then got back n track. "So we'll need to extend that platform at least four feet, support it, and put a railing on both sides then a five-step flight with handrails on both sides—florescent tape on platform and step edges. I'll make a note to backstage lighting that it will need a safety light. You know how dark it usually is back there."

Dan sketched the additions onto the blueprint. "Wait. There isn't the room backstage for those steps to go straight off?" He shuffled to the page that showed the stage dimensions, then back to the blueprint. "They'll have to be angled, like this," and he drew in the stairs at ninety degrees to the platform.

"Looks good," TD agreed.

"So we'll have to add to the lumber list," Dan said as he hooked the tablet into the range of his good hand.

28

"I think that one of the unoccupied floors would be best for the time being," Bruce suggested. "You could then say there was a supervised play area with all the playground equipment like swings and climbing structures. We could photo it up if you needed, but I think that it might be better to send it back to an inspector. If we boxed the space with the planter boxes that were going to that floor anyway, it would enclose the space and even offer a green perimeter. There is bench seating along with the boxes for storytime. Hey, how hard is that? That would work year-round, and you'd still have the river walk if you wanted to take the kids there."

He had obviously outpaced Eustache. "Hey, I'm talking too fast." He attached his credentials and documentation to the letter to the court that Eustache had given him. That letter applied for Eustache to be permitted to visit with his children in a supervised location. "The legal beagles tell me that if the application is accepted, there will be an inspection required, at which time a court-approved body shows up to check up on some things. They need to see where the visit will happen, who will supervise, anything else on their list and then send a report recommending or not. That seems to take a couple of weeks, so we'll have the playground in place before they get here. But they are obliged to come because you applied. So we can do this."

Eustache was getting a bit choked up at the thought of seeing his children again after being denied permission because of his addiction. "Now for the bad news," Bruce said. "The playground stuff will be arriving next week, so you need to ask around for help in installing it. Some assembly will be required. I suggest you get Dan to lay things out and supervise what gets bolted to what. You'll need some buddies to do the assembly; ask at supper time tonight. Once the facility is in place, some of the other guys may be able to use it for visits as well."

When the announcement was made, Bruce amplified it to Jacob, who regularly shared meals with the men, especially supper. "You know, this is going to be a really kick-ass playground, Jake. But if Eustache shows up with his two in that monster space, it will be a bit overwhelming. Do you suppose we might get some of the youngest children from the ladies' tower to come over to play - just to make it look used? If some of the older kids came as helpers to play, push swings, dig in the sandbox, maybe read a story, it could be a much bigger bang for the buck."

"I'll suggest that," said Jacob.

Before Eustache got permission to bring his children, Maggie insisted on approving the facility and only after a personal inspection. She asked Jacob to organize a field trip for children of all ages to test out the equipment. He thought to enlist two moms with infants around a year old because he wanted to get a parent's perspective. It was easy to team up students in his class with the moms for extra support. Edallna had twin, ten-month-old girls. She'd escaped her husband and his family when they found out the twins would be girls and ordered her to have an abortion. Sarina, the other mother, was a teenager herself, scarcely older than students in his class. She, too, had been married against her will and escaped, but not before she found herself pregnant and also facing an ordered abortion of her female fetus.

As soon as the elevator doors opened, they were enveloped in the heady aroma of the wood chips that filled the play area deep enough to pad any tumble. The enclosure was straight off the elevator, but Maggie did an immediate turn to see that the plywood walls around the central container lift were solid and secure. Each ten-year-old was in charge of a preschooler, but it was hard to make that clear when the older kids saw the variety of shiny equipment.

Jacob and Maggie were so engrossed in watching the children they didn't even notice the arrival of Bruce, Pete and Dan. Eustache would be along after work, Bruce said.

"I'm impressed," admitted Jacob. "This looks like any child's dream." The slides and steps attached to the climbing towers were where most of the kids had gathered. Once their charges were safely digging in the sandbox, the older ones were trying out the swinging ropes suspended from the ceiling.

"I'll show you," said Dan to Maggie when she asked about an unfamiliar piece. Dan beckoned Sarina to bring her baby over and strap the infant into the child seat. He directed Mom to sit opposite the infant and gently swing the device. "Just a little bit at first; this is really new to the baby and might be scary. Just a plodding rock and look happy. The infant's eyes never left her mom. Before long, she too was smiling spontaneously - and Mom was overjoyed.

"It's called an expression swing," Dan explained, "and is designed for Mommy to show baby her joy in the experience."

The twins had found the long bench along the play area and the astroturf underfoot was easy enough for them to be walking along, sidestepping, and shouting with excitement.

Maggie was walking around each piece, checking out the dynamics the children were demonstrating, scuffing to see what a falling kid would land on and talking to the mothers about who knew what. Pete was telling anyone who would listen to the make and model of each piece. Dan was explaining how the arcs of motion of anything moveable had been carefully measured to be sure kids didn't collide. It was some time before Jacob noticed there didn't seem to be as many children as he'd come with. The preschoolers were accounted for; where were their young minders? It only took a glance past the potted trees to see them. Someone had brought a ball, and they were using the vast open space on the rest of the floor to play soccer.

Those who were tired of waiting for the ball were playing tag. A couple had just found the floor was circular, and they could run all the way around.

Maggie followed his gaze. "There is something perverse about children getting as much fun out of a five-dollar ball as out of a fifty thousand dollar playground."

Jacob turned her to look at the rest of the kids. "They aren't playing ball."

At that moment, they both spotted one of the twins staring across the space between the bench she was standing against, and the next one, just two steps away. The child let go and was teetering on both feet, then one moved, and the other, and she was across.

"For some reason, that makes my day," Jacob said.

Mom had also witnessed the moment of her child's first unsupported step from a distance. Her hands were in front of her face, and she was laughing so hard she had tears.

"Watch," Jacob said before Maggie could run over and hug Edallna. The twin had turned to look at her sister, now at the place where she had been moments before.

"Da. Da. Da," the first twin chatted, patting her new support and looking back. Number two stood looking across the space. Mom had knelt, so she was also in the second child's line of sight and silently held out her hands and nodded. Number two stepped out, swayed and regained her balance. But now, she was stuck midway with no momentum to carry her forward. Mom reached out further with one hand, and the baby touched it and took the next step that got her to the new bench. All the adults clapped. Nobody noticed that Eustache had arrived.

"I didn't notice you," Jacob said. "We were watching that little drama," and he waved to the twins, now sidestepping through new territory.

"I saw them."

"Your team did an excellent job on the playground. Just listen to the happiness. It warms a heart like mine. I hope you are proud and will tell the others what a great job they did."

"If it gets me time with my kids again, it will be worth anything. In fact, they'll... Here they are now. I asked them to come by on the way to happy hour when I heard you had a dry run."

Five men stepped out of the elevator and moved towards them. Dan turned and greeted them, but the moms instinctively stepped in front of their children and slid sideways behind Maggie, whether it was their sudden and unannounced arrival. When the soccer ball shot across their path, the child chasing it stopped and stared. The children in the playground played on, oblivious.

Dan introduced the men and explained their role in the project. There were neutral nods from the mothers. Maggie complimented them enthusiastically. One of the men asked if someone could demonstrate the expression swing. The baby who was placed in it with Mom recognized the situation and was waving excitedly.

"Couldn't imagine that," the man said. "And you can swing sideways as well as back and forth. Interesting." Plainly, he was pleased with the toy he'd helped install. The men drifted apart, trying not to intrude. One pointed to an eyebolt he'd installed in the ceiling as a child ran and grabbed the rope hanging from it and swung in an arc. His mate was watching the two children chasing each other out of the crawl tube. "I put that together," he bragged. They called out to Dan that they were going. Jacob knew what the talk would be in the lounge tonight.

"I hope you brought a story," Maggie said. "It is time to settle these kids down before we go to dinner."

Pete corrected her. "It's supper. Dinner is at mid-day."

"Pardon?" Maggie replied.

"Local peculiarity," Jacob said and held up his book of nursery rhymes that he still had from his days as a church minister. "Could you call up the kids, Dan?" Dan pursed his lips and gave a piercing steam-whistle blast that stopped everyone. They were all called back and directed into the corner of the play area. Some sat on the wood chips. Jacob was trying to figure where he would stand to read his poetry sermon when Eustache tugged at his sleeve.

"Could I do a story that my Dad did for me when I

was that age?"

This was not part of the plan, and Jacob winced inside.

"I brought my costume," Eustache said, pointing to his gym bag.

"*Well, if it flops, I still have my book,*" Jacob thought. He made the call.

"Sure. What is the story about?"

"The fox and the crow. It takes about five minutes."

Jacob strode to the centre of the group and called for their attention. When that didn't work, he held up his hand. It was the signal for them all to do the same and stop talking.

"It is almost time for us to go home, but before we go, we have a special story from the man who inspired and helped build this playground. He said the story is about a fox and a crow. A fox is a sly, clever animal with orangey fur, and it looks like a dog. You all know what a crow looks like, right? Big, black, bird?" The children nodded. "OK, Eustache, you're on."

He turned but could not see the other man. Instead, a raucous squawking came from the playhouse at the top of the climbing toy beside them. Flapping at the top of the slide was a crouched figure covered in a voluminous black cloak. A helmeted mask with a long black beak and beady eyes gave the figure a sort of sinister but mischievous look. It flapped and cawed enough to get everyone's attention, and then into the silence, a crackly voice said.

"Maître Corbeau, sur un arbre perché" followed by more cawing and flapping.

"What did he say?" Questions of all sorts tumbled over each other. Through it, all cut Alisha's voice. She was one of Jacob's senior students who had come to care for the young ones.

"It's a French poem. Just watch," but she started to translate anyway. "Master Crow was perched on a tree, and he was..."

"Tenait en son bec un fromage." The crow cackled somehow despite the round chunk that had appeared in the bird's beak.

"...holding a cheese in his beak," said Alisha.

A theatrical prancing about by the bird accompanied the children's telling each other that the chunk was cheese like they had for lunch. In a blink, the bird disappeared down the crawl tube slide that led the other way instead of the open slide that came towards them. But out of the slide did not come the black bird. What emerged was a figure in an orange fur cape with a helmet that looked like a smiling dog. Everyone exclaimed at the transformation, but it was cut short by Eustache's penetrating and slow voice.

"Maître Renard, par l'odeur alléché." The figure was

moving his head back and forth, nose raised as Alisha translated,

"Master Fox attracted by the smell said:"

"Lui tint à peu près ce langage :
Hé ! bonjour, Monsieur du Corbeau."

"Well, Hello, Mister Crow!" as the figure cavorted about sniffing and finally coming to centre stage. His voice was now smooth and silky.

"Que vous êtes joli ! que vous me semblez beau !
Sans mentir, si votre ramage,
Se rapporte à votre plumage,
Vous êtes le Phénix des hôtes de ces bois."

"He's telling the crow that he is a really pretty bird and that if he could sing as beautifully as he looks, he'd be the most beautiful bird in the forest," Alisha explained. She had not stopped before the orange figure whirled like a ballerina and spun across to the other side of the space and stopped enclosed in black again. The dog's nose was now a beak again. Some of the older children were not deceived. They saw that the helmet was really two-faced and that the fox's face was now pointing away and almost covered by the black cloak. But the black beak held the big cheese they had seen earlier.

"Where did it come from?" one asked.

"Shhh."

"A ces mots le Corbeau ne se sent pas de joie ;
Et pour montrer sa belle voix,
Il ouvre un large bec, laisse tomber sa proie."

"The crow was so flattered and believed the fox. In order to show off his beautiful voice, He opened his beak wide,"

With a horrible squawk, the crow threw back his head and spun like a dervish. The cheese flew up in the air, and all eyes followed it. When it was caught, it was the orange-cloaked fox with his sly smile who snatched it on the other side of the space. Amazed exclamations were cut off by the narrator.

"Le Renard s'en saisit, et dit : «Mon bon Monsieur,
Apprenez que tout flatteur,
Vit aux dépens de celui qui l'écoute :
Cette leçon vaut bien un fromage, sans doute.»"

Alisha kept up her translation. "The fox says: 'My good man, learn that every flatterer will take your lunch if you believe them'. It cost the crow his cheese."

The figure spun again and came to a stop now, dressed in black. The body language said how sad the bird was and rubbed an eye that would have had tears.

"Le Corbeau, honteux et confus,
Jura, mais un peu tard, qu'on ne l'y prendrait plus.

"The crow was really sad," Alisha explained as the figure stamped an angry foot, "and said that he would not

TO GIVE AND RECEIVE WITH GRACE

be tricked again." As she said this, the figure pulled off his cloak with a swirl that revealed its reversible quality, and his mask that swung on a pivot on a skullcap and bowed deeply.

The adults applauded loudly, "Bravo," shouted Jacob, and all the children joined in. Jacob rose in place and thanked Eustache ending with "Merci beaucoup," which exhausted his French vocabulary. Everyone applauded more, and departure was announced.

The children repeatedly asked if they could come again. A couple of the older ones approached Eustache and asked if they could put on his cloak. He showed them how to put their hands into the pockets on the hem to control it better. Others examined the clever helmet mask.

"How do you know French, Alisha?" another asked.

"We speak French at home."

"But you don't speak French in class?"

"With who? Do you speak French?" The child shook his head. "Would you like to learn?"

"Yes," said the child. They walked towards the elevator, chatting small talk.

Jacob said that he'd go out with the children when the other men said they'd head up to the lounge. Some of the younger children occupied the older ones asking why the fox didn't share the cheese and was sushed because the babies were asleep. Explanations had to go on in whispers.

"I think I'd call that a success," Maggie acknowledged. The mums agreed. When they went ahead as they crossed the parking lot to Lindsay Tower, Maggie pointed out it might be a way to get children used to adult men and maybe some of the women themselves. "One more step along the way we go," she sang quietly. "I didn't think you knew hymns," Jacob responded. "Good lyrics for most of it," she replied. "I never cease to be impressed at the talent that stereotypes bury," Maggie said as she left them to go to her office. "It shouldn't be necessary, but it is good to be reminded every day."

Jacob delivered all his charges to their cafeteria then headed back to the end of Happy Hour with the men. He hoped he'd still be in time for an ale.

\*

Eustache was the centre of attention. When Jacob walked in, he was demonstrating to the others how dancers spin without getting dizzy. Bruce had the beer he'd called ahead for and sank into the chair he pulled out for him.

"Over the fence home run," Jacob complimented. "This opens up a whole new option for the community. Are there other men who might like to reconnect with their children and use the playground as a venue?" he asked.

"That's three questions," Pete chided. "Yes, there are other men who have children and possibly they might want to reunite with them. But maybe the children don't want to see their father. The last question about using the playground to meet children would depend on their age, I would guess."

"Pete. That reply is the icing on today's cake. I don't recall the last time I heard you talk so much about anything."

"Thank you." He looked down, but when Bruce cleared his throat, he looked up. "I've been practicing with Bruce. I'm learning to say what I was thinking, but I was afraid to speak up before." He looked down again.

Jacob reached for Pete's shoulder. Pete jumped a bit at the touch, looked at the hand, and then up into Jacob's face. "Pete, you are a remarkable man. I know you served your country in Afghanistan and almost died during that time. I've seen you struggle back, and here you sit. I can't say how proud you make me feel to have known you. Your face belongs on a poster. You inspire us all. Please, don't ever forget that. You are a model we can all look up to."

"Thank you, Jake," he said as he flashed a glance at Bruce before looking Jacob full on. From the corner of his eye, Jacob caught the grin that disappeared behind Bruce's glass as he raised it for a sip.

Jacob's ecclesiastical credentials were not enough to get him appointed as a court supervisor of Eustache's visiting with his children, but Bruce's social work experience got him the job. Jacob could organize a field trip for preschoolers from his place, so Eustache's children had company. Pete was there as part of his social revitalizing plan. It was all rather complicated, but it was working.

Eustache's wife had come for the initial handover, as it were. It was a brittle few moments that Jacob had smoothed as best he could when the layout and procedure were confirmed. Bruce made a show of setting his watch timer and specifying the pickup point downstairs in the lobby. Pete escorted her down in the elevator as she saw no need for her own elevator pass to the playground floor. Being photographed to come up and check out the situation had been enough of a hassle. Before she left, Jacob renewed the possibility of getting her own pass later. He avoided saying how much Eustache had been looking forward to the day. She made clear she was only there to do what the court ordered, and she'd be back on time. He'd better be also.

Pete was back with the news that it was a silent trip and the observation that she seemed to be an irate woman. It surprised Jacob to hear that sort of response from Pete.

Bruce asked what Pete had observed to lead to that conclusion and got a list. "You have an amazing ability to note minutiae. That is your strength," he said. What all that stuff means is what you are getting better at. Well done, soldier."

"Eustache brought some new mini cars," Pete noted, and they all turned toward the man playing with his children in the sandbox. Half a dozen of Jacob's group was also highly involved. TD had offered cutoffs from the woodshop to work as buildings and bridges. They all seemed to be making roads and interchanges. Fortunately, Pete had brought extra cars.

Pete named off the makes and models. "The wheels will jam up with the sand," he went on.

Bruce continued his teaching. "Those are expensive toys. It must mean a lot to Eustache to have them so he can play with his kids even if it damages the cars."

"So it's a tradeoff?"

"Yep, and everybody would see it differently. That's why social things are so hard. But you're getting it."

"He should wash the cars off in a bucket and then pour the bucket on the plants," Pete persisted.

"Would you like to suggest it to him?"

"He might say no."

"But he might say 'yes,' and then you would have helped him and his children to preserve the cars. It's a tradeoff."

"I'm going to try," Pete declared after a moment, and he got up to bring the pail from the water spout that was used to water the planting boxes.

As he was going and facing that way, Bruce stood and stretched theatrically. The movement caught Eustache's attention. Bruce just tipped his head towards Pete, now at the tap, and sat down.

Jacob watched the washing play out until Bruce's alarm went off. He stood again, and the shrug of Eustache's shoulder's said it all. "Time for you kids to go," Eustache announced. "Maybe we can do this again sometime."

"Awww. Do we have to go already?" the kids groaned in chorus.

"Yep. Let's go. Bruce is calling. Your mum will be downstairs."

"Here's your cars back, sir," said a couple of Jacob's group. "We like your cars. Can you come again?"

"Hope so," he said as he asked his kids to hold the wet cars as he dumped the water into the planting box. The kids put the wet toys in Eustache's backpack as they waited for the elevator. He took one out for each child. They were drying them on their T-shirt tails as the door closed.

"Your idea was a good one, Pete," Jacob complimented.

"Thanks."

After several companionable moments of silence watching the children, now on the climbing toy and swing since the cars had gone. Jacob asked, "How do you remember the numbers of everything?"

"I don't know. It makes me sad when I find other people don't remember numbers like I do. I feel like I don't belong." The silence thickened before he went on. "But I don't spell names and things well. I was happy when I found things have numbers so I could remember them then."

"That's amazing," Jacob said. "You remind me of an ancient philosopher. He was a brilliant man, too. He saw mathematics in everything. I'll bet you and him would have got on well." And then, on a whim that he regretted later, he asked Pete, "What's the model number of that expression swing the mums love over there?" He was smiling then.

"Three, three, two."

"How do you know that?" His smile broadened. This was amazing.

"It was half the pass number of the guy who got knocked off the floor as they put the windows in. Sid Oleskew was his name, but I couldn't write any of their names well, so I used the last numbers of anyone's site pass. His was six, six, four, and he was knocked off this floor, over there. He hooked his finger to the other side of the building. Pete went on to explain the patterns in the codes and..." He went on to give the number of other pieces on the playground and how he recalled them.

Jacob felt sick.

"Did you say that people used site pass numbers to identify each other when we were building this place?" He could hardly get the words out.

"Sure," said Pete. "It's so much better than their names. Like Blake and Byron, the twins? Each has his own pass number. I don't get mixed up..." Jacob turned away. All he was thinking about was the moment he saw that three-digit number on that hundred dollar bill in TD's wallet. The number might be argued as a random one, but it could also be tied to a particular person on the worksite. He'd bet a dollar to a donut that the numbers on the bills found on Tank would also have a name from the building site attached to them also.

Jacob collected the children and got them all back to their lounge for supper with the help of his student chaperones and the two moms. But all he could think of as he moved everyone along was the addition of yet another coincidence in the case of the disappearance of Austin Zid. At what point were there too many?

29

How do you ask a friend if he's a killer? It hadn't been part of the conversation skills class in his pastoral training. So Jacob sat, mind a-churning, watching the children play in the sandbox with the collection of additional end cuts that TD had brought from the woodshop. Today, both men were Eustache's co-supervisors for the supervised visits the court had allowed him with his children. If anyone asked, TD's name for the moment was 'Bruce,' who was the actual court designate, but Bruce was busy rescuing another soul at that moment. He was expected soon.

"Did you ever see anyone having so much fun?" Jacob finally asked. Neither of Eustache's watchers had had children - Jacob by biology, TD by choice. "I wonder if he'll ever be able to see them without a minder?"

"Maybe not. It depends on how forgiving the others are of his drug habit and whether they really believe the rehab reports." New roads were being scrapped out in the sand with plywood scraps. Other children from the group Jacob had brought asked to join in the play.

"Could you make us a parking lot for all these cars over here?" Eustache asked. "Here are some scrapers."

"Can I build the road over to the buildings?" another asked. The buildings would rise from the jumble of wooden chunks brought up from the scrap bin in the carpentry shop. Anyone could see that.

"We need a mountain for the trees," Eustache suggested, and a parking lot builder called her friends to join. In no time, half a dozen were creating a new world.

The mums with the one-year-olds that had come with Jacob were guiding their toddlers up the steps to the small slide.

In the midst of such excitement and joy, Jacob thought he heard TD grind his teeth.

"We used to build mock-ups like that when we were planning an operation in Afghanistan." TD said tightly. "It didn't matter how many high-tech photos we had; some of the guys just had to build a model. Just like that." He shivered involuntarily. "Where the hell is Bruce? He was supposed to be here by now. I just brought up scraps for the kids to play with. I didn't think I'd have to watch my life's rerun."

Jacob knew the ghosts of the mission in which TD had lost all but one of his patrol in an ambush had risen, unbidden. It was not the first time he'd heard the story.

"He said he'd be along shortly. Thanks for taking his place for Eustache's benefit. These visits mean the world to him."

They sat in silence as the sandbox metropolis took shape in front of them. "You never think that when you sign up, that it will ever get to you," TD said, struggling to gain control. "They give you a gun and a license to kill and train you in a dozen ways to do it. It's all so manly, so heroic, this destiny you're helping to create. It's like some big game. You have the controller, and you move the figures around. BOOM! SMASH! And you all have a laugh and go for a beer. Nobody ever tells you what it's like to see your companions mowed down, what it's like to be covered in their blood and guts and wondering why the bullets missed you. It makes you feel so… angry," his fist clenched, "…and sad all at once." He tipped his head back and drew deep breaths.

"I think that is how Austin Zid must have made you feel." Jacob should have been more sensitive, but the words slipped out from beneath the veneer, covering his own turmoil.

"Who?"

231

"That guy who worked for the contractors who build this place. You and Pete scooped his lunch box once and gave it to Detective Winters."

"That guy was vermin," TD replied with a swipe of his hand. With his colour rising, he went on to list the abuse he'd inflicted on Pete and the victimizing of fellow employees by making them pay protection money and trafficking drugs. "He was a bully and a social parasite. He deserved what he got."

TD sat back but then turned again. He struggled to keep his voice under the cheerful voices beyond. "Don't go all religious on me by trying to say he was one of God's creatures and will meet his judgement later. You know as well as I do that it is fiction. I've heard you say it time and again. Life-threatening germs and predatory animals have no place in human society. I've seen what you do with a bottle of disinfectant. I heard you talk about snakes. I know the vicious control that others meted out on you for seeking enlightenment. All life is not equal. Zid was cancer on all about him, and I know what you think of cancer - like the one that took your wife."

Jacob felt like he'd been sucker-punched.

"Here's Bruce," TD said, looking past Jacob. "I can go now." He leapt up and strode off towards the stairs instead of the elevator.

"That looked confrontational," Bruce said as he sat down.

"I feel like my whole life is falling apart.... again." Jacob moaned.

"Well, the doctor is in for fifteen minutes, by which time you have to take your mob home, and I need to surrender E's kids to their keeper. Talk fast."

His attempt at levity fell flat.

Jacob poured out, to Bruce, the new reasons he believed TD had killed Zid.

"We sent over this back a while ago," Bruce reminded him of the night he'd come at Jacob's call to deal with the coroner's report. "You want TD to tell you he killed a man so that you can turn him over to the police?"

"Isn't that the right thing?"

"And go to prison and never be seen here again."

"If that is what a court decides."

"A jury of his peers would decide his guilt?"

"That's the way it's set up."

"Jacob, look around. Where do you think he is? Is a downtown court with a jury, you imagine, better than this one? Could any single one of those presumed fair-minded citizens, let alone all of them in a jury, claim to have been in battle? He's living and working with another jury here every day. If you were curious about how these guys, his peers, might react to the charge that TD killed Zid, I'd say they'd hold him a celebration party. Zid was a mean hombre, from what I heard. I know how terrified Pete was of him and why."

Eustache was looking at his watch and spoke to the children. It looked like he was suggesting the kids wash up the cars.

"So let's imagine that some other jury did decide TD was guilty. We know where that goes. Instead of that, let's imagine another sentence - to here. A group of his peers is watching him, even working with and under him. So which do you suppose will produce the best outcome?

Jacob was stunned. "But you can't go around killing people. If TD killed that man, there is a process that has to be followed to find out if he did, and if so, to pass judgement.

"Well, from the process that you described, that has already taken place. He has not been found to have killed the man. I'm not saying he wasn't paid to kill others earlier. That is not the issue. If you are concerned about others you are associating with who have killed people, Pete, myself and several others in the building should be on your list. Jacob, if you are looking for an absolute here, I'd suggest it is in the same category as those other theological ones that you just abandoned."

"I think it's time to go," Eustache said as he approached.

Jake felt jerked back to the real world. The mums had the babies all back in their carriages.

"Time to corral your kids, Jake."

Jacob shook his head. "Line up," he called.

"Can I count everybody?" asked a small voice.

"No me," called another.

Jake asked each to count separate rows.

"Can I call the elevator?" Two had to press the button together.

30

Jacob's abandonment of theological absolutes had been a liberating experience. It had left him feeling that the critical fact that bound people together was their humanity, and the compassion is required of all. But he hadn't counted on that expression of care ever confronting the killing of someone.

As he walked home, it was the fact that he hadn't imagined this conflict that bothered him. How could he have not seen that this fundamental could pass unexamined? His earlier thinking seemed so simplistic now. He'd abandoned the religion in which he'd been so deeply rooted and thought he'd found a more transcendent level. But it had brought him to this impasse.

As he thought, it looked like generations of thinkers before him had done the same and opted for the religious solution as the simplest one to implement. It grew out of empires that sought control and order in the pursuit of whatever else they sought. Those thinkers had codified behaviours that were acceptable or not and established the punishment for deviance from that practice. The search for right behaviour had been called justice and careers over millennia had been devoted to its accomplishment. But that whole pursuit now seemed just a means to an end, a substitute whole, a pretence.

The reading that had liberated Jacob theologically had been unnerving too. It brought him up short when it led him to an article about how hunter-gatherer societies now, and possibly in Neanderthal communities before writing was invented, dealt with abusive members. There were limits on who could demand how much from the community. When you crossed that line enough to be a threat, what did they do?

The researcher had concluded that members of those communities exiled or exterminated aberrant members after a long discussion. That sounded like a jury system. He wondered who delivered the news or the punishment. Was it a mob scene, say like the one who ended the rule of Julius Caesar? Wasn't Brutus a friend the day before he led the attack? Those assassins were lauded as heroes at the time, as he recalled. Did any one of those men face a trial? Justice? He couldn't find that record.

So if TD killed Zid, did he, as a leader, have the right or duty to exterminate the threats that Zid represented? Zid had had the warning to change what he did. He ignored the message, even flaunted his continued abuse. Bruce had suggested that protection of the greater good of the community foundation was more important than the absolute Jacob had been sanctifying.

Going back to his historical parallel, he wondered if Caesar was on the wrong end of a political struggle, and it was those who came to power with new political priorities that thought their actions were justified - if not even the will of the Gods. His death wasn't about justice at all; it was a settling of political scores and wrapping the actions up in some divine or elemental reason.

That thought made him feel like he was getting back on his mental feet. This 'right and wrong' thing was really a political measure of behaviour. It could be dressed up in religious rationale and robes, but that is still what it was. He'd rescued Brian from a vest that was meant to explode and punish his mother for her demands for individuality. She was supposed to obey her husband without question. When she didn't, she had to be put in her place by destroying what she valued most. Well, that was a religious/political expression of the society from which she sought to escape. His feeling that he was getting somewhere in balancing behaviour against belief was getting back on track. He suddenly realized he'd walked past his own house, completely oblivious.

He started to retrace his steps and found that the act of turning the physical corner had produced a mental turn as well. It was more than sad that anyone, even Zid, had died. Surely others knew and loved him. If TD had murdered him, it was also a tragedy, but the practice seemed to be a fact of humanity. TD was acting out a fundamental approach that went way back.

When pushed beyond limits, people act. Trying to second-guess the reasons or rationale seemed to be another feature of human behaviour impelled by the group to which you belonged and the threat imposed by what you acted against. The words in his mind seemed to be spinning out as though he was back in his pulpit - more comfortable with each step.

So when any action was evaluated by those not there, it seemed to change the question. The jurors were looking for objective fairness that really didn't exist any more than did the deity upon which the witnesses took an oath. They were following something made up of different parts punishment, tradition, universality, and implementation - with a dash of humanity maybe. The product was then called justice, but it was only for that society, for that place, for that time.

If the mix increased the humanity portion, it had to decrease the relative amounts of the rest, but it could still do the right thing for that new place and time and with this new community. Surely a mother or wife or sibling might have sought justice or vengeance. Zid was their kin. They felt it was right to see that the person who killed their loved one was punished. Right!

If Zid was just an employee of another group who felt extortion was their right, they might not want the oppressed to imagine freedom. They might return to impress their own sense of rightness. They would relish the sight of punishment being meted out on anyone who would lead their victims to think they could get away with freedom. Great to see the state dish out the penalty. It would send more of a message than if they did it themselves. Keep straight who was really in charge.

And that led him slowly, but with increasing confidence, to frame his action into words. He looked up to see his front door. As he searched for his key, he realized he was being challenged like never before. If giving or accepting with grace was not enough, then…

He felt himself slide mentally backwards when he thought his response was one of forgiving. There it was again. That absolute, rearing up for dominance. You can only forgive if you have the moral high ground. There was no such space. Forgetting was not an option either. It diminished the event by doing so. He poked the key into the lock. Didn't fit. Confused, he looked down at the back door key he was trying to push into the front door lock.

"God damned right," he thought, and he didn't even shiver at the wording. It was wrong to kill someone… unless you and your group held a value closer to what humanity meant. If that adversary would see any one of you slain for their private gain, it was the pursuit of the personal that they represented. If you felt the group was more important, of course, you were at odds with them. And if nothing else worked, well...

There was the key he wanted. It zipped into the lock with a satisfying shiver. He unlocked the door and felt the familiar scents of home swirl out to meet him.

So what was it he was called to practice? The self-satisfaction of superiority involved in being forgiving or forgetting still clung to him like aftershave. But with the resolve it takes to wash the smell away, he searched for another response.

Forbearance. That was it. That had the elements he was looking for. You did not have to condone. You could still disagree, but you found within yourself the ability to accept, endure, and carry on. Yeah, he liked that. He looked up, surprised to find himself in his kitchen, and he hadn't closed the door.

He kicked it closed behind him and hooked his hat on the rack. "Yeah," he thought. "Forbearance sounds good enough."

PANDAMONIUMPUBLISHING.COM
PANDAPUBLISHING8@GMAIL.COM

www.ingramcontent.com/pod-product-compliance
Lightning Source LLC
Chambersburg PA
CBHW020359030726
47496CB00007B/2211